MW01244100

EDDIE'S JOURNEY

'A Special Read for the Rescue Dog Lovers'

TRACY ROESCH WILLIAMS

Copyright © 2022
Tracy Roesch Williams
Eddie's Journey
'A Special Read for the Rescue Dog Lovers'
All rights reserved.

No part of this publication may be reproduced, distributed, or
transmitted in any form or by any means, including photocopying,
recording, or other electronic or mechanical methods, without the prior
written permission of the publisher, except in the case of brief
quotations embodied in critical reviews and certain other non-
commercial uses permitted by copyright law.

Tracy Roesch Williams

Printed in the United States of America
First Printing 2022
First Edition 2022

ISBN 979-8-9861149-0-3

10 9 8 7 6 5 4 3 2 1

Front Photo Credit: David Jensen Photography

EDDIE'S JOURNEY

TABLE OF CONTENTS

INTRODUCTION

Eddie's story came to be about 10 years ago when I felt this intuitive need for his story to be heard. As one of his humans, my hope is to convey a story of overcoming difficulties, abandonment, sadness, and welcoming LOVE into life.

If a dog named Eddie can overcome these challenges, there is hope for each of us.

CHAPTER 1

ME

I am Eddie the Dog. I was born in 2008. I live in the now, and have trouble remembering the past, so I will start with my day today. I learned quickly that I was born unique. My very first memory is a feeling of, well, feeling "different than". I am told that my parents were a Corgi and an American Staffordshire Terrier. I have felt comfortable in my body from the beginning. However, many humans seem to have interesting comments on my body.

Various comments are made every day of my life, i.e.: his head is huge, he must have lots of brains, look at his funny body, what on earth is he? (this is the most common), he looks like a cartoon character, he is funky, WOW, he is all boy, what an interesting dog, midget, little man, mixed breed, laughter when they see me, how old is he, he is unforgettable. I know my name to be, He, Little Man, Eddie, Eddie Bear..mostly I listen in when I hear 'he'. I am who I am and that is ok. I also ignore most humans that are overly aggressive or have a funny smell. I like little people the best.

I am living in a bit of a chaotic home. I know the humans love me the best they can. There is lots of yelling happening today and it seems to happen every day. Each day I wake, I think today may be different. I hide in the safest spots so as to not get yelled at when I am underfoot. I am currently getting yelled at and told to go lay down. I am sad and will seek comfort with the cat. I think she feels the same way. She lets me snuggle close to her and I like that. I am hopeful that I will not get beaten today. I am confused because I tried to make the humans happy. I want them to be happy. I love them. The man human is screaming 'Eddie COME here now'! I hustle as fast as I can and yet it is not fast enough as he is standing there yelling at me. Out the door, we go! He scolds me and tells me to get in the truck. My stomach hurts. I jump as high as I can, hoping to end up in the front seat and not on the ground. It is so far up. Darn it! I land on the ground. Oh no!!! He is grabbing me by my neck, 'Damn you, Eddie, are you stupid?' This hurts my neck ....

"Yipe"!"

"Oh shut up!" he says! He tosses me onto the seat. I slink away quickly from him. I am so sorry. I hate to disappoint him.

Off we go. I keep my head down and grip my pads into the seat as we whirl around curves and twists. I balance as best I can. I am determined to stay in my seat. I am determined not to make eye contact with him.

He gets out of the car and starts grabbing his stuff from the truck. He is loud and clanking his things around. He is speaking loudly, and I can tell he is angry. I cringe and hope I can stay here.

I will be very quiet and maybe he will forget about me. He is still loud and pulls the handle on his machine. He yells. He pulls it again and again and again. Then he throws something in the air. It lands in the back of the truck loudly and I jump. He pulls and pulls and pulls and finally, his little engine ignites. I feel relief. I hate that machine because it makes him so angry all the time. He goes up and down people's lawns. Some people come out of their homes, and he yells at them. That machine is bad.

Here is what I remember about what happened...

I was finally left at a place called Animal Control when the humans could no longer give me any attention. I was so very sad and knew that I had done something wrong to be left there. I tried, I tried hard to be a good boy. I always felt like I was letting them down. When the man human would start yelling or hitting me, I would get very quiet and try to hide from him.

Mostly my first home is a blur to me.

I was adopted after some time by my second family where I lived for a few years. The man human loved me so much. The female human tried to love me, but I knew deep inside she did not. She felt threatened by her husband's love for me. He would pay extra special attention to me and play ball with me.

There were little ones in the house. I loved them. I loved to make them giggle and I snuggled with the littlest one often. I also liked the cat. The human man was gone often and would put on a uniform before leaving. Sometimes he would be gone for what seemed like forever. I would be sad when he left as the human lady could not give me much attention. There were little ones and things to do with them. Sometimes I would not get fed even though I tried to remind her to feed me. Again, I tried to be quiet and not get in the way as I did not want to have to go away again.

Then the day came. I saw it coming and wished I would have done something to stop it from happening. It was so confusing what was going on. I saw things being thrown in boxes. All of our things are in boxes. There was some arguing. The lady started getting sick in the mornings. I worried about her, however later in the day she seemed ok, it was just the mornings that she seemed to not feel good. There was talk of leaving Alaska. I was not sure what that meant. At one point I saw him packing a separate bag from the ones for the rest of the family. All of his fancy uniforms were getting put in duffle bags with nothing from the rest of the family. I felt so much confusion and sleepless nights.

All my things got put in a bag......my heart started beating very fast. What was happening? It seemed so quick and yet time was standing still. I was paralyzed. The little one was hugging me and sobbing uncontrollably. The lady kept saying goodbye - Dad has to leave now. The next thing I knew, I was in the car like always with my human Dad, and he was crying.

I tried to make him laugh like he always did with me. He had told me things that were private, personal things, throughout our time together and I tried to get him to talk to me. He would not. He hardly looked at me, just drove and cried. We stopped and he looked at me and said, Eddie, I will never forget you. I love you so very much. I have to go away. I promise I will come back. His tears fell all over me. I was soaked. I was crying too. Don't leave me Dad...please, I promise to be a good boy. Don't leave me.

He took me out of the car and into this building where they took me. He turned and walked away. WAIT!!!!! DAD! WAIT!!! Where are you going? DAD?! Wait!!!! He never looked back. He was gone.

The place put me in a kennel. I had room to roam and walk outside, but it felt very cold and lonely. I was terrified. I wondered why I was being punished. I tried to be a good boy. I missed my human Dad so much already.

They fed me, but I refused to eat. My stomach hurt and I had diarrhea. I did not want to eat, I wanted to go home to my pack, my humans.

There was this feeling I was getting from another dog. It was the strangest thing as the dog was not in the kennel with me and all the other dogs. It was as if it was speaking through me inside my mind. It baffled me and I would ignore it, however, it would reappear in my head. It told me that I was going to be ok and that two humans were going to love me so very much. The voice, head chatter, whatever you want to call it told me that it was moving away from these two humans very soon and that I was needed in their lives to love them and help them move on from their loss.

Again…it was an odd time and the days seemed to all blur together….the head chatter did not seem real nor did the whole experience. I felt like I was in a dream - a bad dream, and I would awake soon to find that it was a dream. I would be back in my home with my Dad, and my human family, loving on my little human girl. Ohhh she loved me so much. But when? When would I awake from this nightmare?

The only comfort this whole time was this gentle loving voice. Although as I said, I tried ignoring it, it was like a warm blanket offering me peace and comfort.

There was so much noise. Barking and carrying on all the time, day and night. One of the girls that seemed to be in charge was so nice to me. She said the nicest things and asked me why I would not eat? I did not want to like her, so I would often walk away from her.

On certain days of the week, strangers would arrive. That is when the place got extremely loud and annoying. I was put in another kennel so I could not see what was going on out where all the strangers wandered in. I knew it was a bad scene as many of the dogs that I was getting to know and a few I liked would be gone once the strangers left. This was not comforting at all. It seemed we were all very confused, and we all felt like we were bad dogs.

The second time this happened I asked one of my friends that was out in the commotion if he knew what happened. I also asked why he was still here? He said droves of humans visited. The cute dogs were given new homes with these humans. He said the humans especially liked the puppies and ....well, the cuter dogs. He said he knew he was not a cute dog. He had never been told how adorable or cuddly or smart or any of the words that he heard the nice lady at the kennel tell these humans. He was a 'lesser' dog and he knew it. I did not know what to say to him. He said he watched the others turn it on. They used what we called 'cute face' or cute body movements to get the human's attention. To get new homes. We were all fending for ourselves and had to do whatever it took to get out of where we were.

There were rumors that dogs like us that were 'bad' often did not make it out alive. This hurts my heart and upsets my stomach. I was starting to get very skinny. Still, there was the voice telling me...."There is a plan.....be patient."

One day I was hanging with a nice lady. She was grooming some dogs and tending to many. There was a ringing noise and I saw her pick up that odd thing that humans talk into. She said my human Dad's name. I could hear his voice on the other end of the phone. I was so very excited!!! My whole body started wagging and I jumped on her lap with my front paws. She giggled and said, "Eddie knows it is you on the other end. He is so excited right now."

I wanted to crawl through that thing that she had up to her ear and get to him!!! I had so many questions for him, mostly where are you and when can I come home?

The nice lady looked right into my eyes and got quiet. She said, "oh....emmm, aha, I see, I am very sorry, we will take good care of him and find him his forever home" .....I slid down to the floor. I am not sure I wanted to understand what just happened, but her face told me everything. He was not coming back to get me. I felt sick. I wanted to cry but had to remain strong. I was so very sorry for whatever I had done for this to happen. I had thought he loved me. I know I loved him. I was so confused right now. My head was spinning.

The voice that I had come to find comfort in had left my head within the last week. I missed it and wanted it to talk to me now more than ever, but it did not. Where did that voice go and what the heck was it? Maybe I had been hallucinating.

Now what? I know, I would starve myself. That would be the ultimate punishment for me and whatever I had done to be put here.

The nice lady offered scratches. She did not know my favorite spots as he did. I did not want to make her angry, so I sat there letting her touch me. I was frozen in pain. I would never love again or eat again, so she could touch me all she wanted. She talked to me too, although I had no idea what she was saying, and I didn't care.

Days seemed to blend. There were always new dogs appearing and a few others leaving. I kept to myself so as to not make any new friends because I knew my heart would get broken. My lessor friend has been a constant. He got to go home once in a while with the nice lady.

There was talk amongst the nice lady and others of strangers coming that night. It was cold outside. My starving hadn't killed me yet. I was very thin and felt cold all the time. Often, I would sit and shiver.

As the nice lady hustled about getting ready for the strangers to appear she did what she always did with me, moved me inside away from the strangers and chaos. I was in a separate secluded area, although I could hear lots of noise, barking.

I was snuggled tight trying to warm my bones and heard the commotion start. The nice lady appeared just as I was dozing off.

She said, "Come on Eddie, I have a feeling tonight is your night!" I had no clue what she was referring to and followed her down the hallway.

She put me in a kennel in the area with all the commotion. All the other dogs were barking loudly, and strangers were looking in our kennels. I was annoyed and so I ignored them. I looked away when they looked at me. I was disgusted. I knew it from the tip of my toes that I was a bad boy... a lessor.

Something happened....Some odd feeling happened. That voice that was in my head...well it wasn't in my head, but it felt like it was around me. It was the strangest feeling, and I am not sure I can describe it to you. It was a pull, a warmth, a smell, a noise, love ...NO! NO...I will never love again....but this pull.

I heard a girl's voice, "We are here to see the puppies" and then....then.....there was this man looking at me. I tried my hardest to turn away from him. There was this pull - this thing that had been in my head was in his eyes. It pulled my soul. My eyes bared into his eyes...for what seemed like an eternity we were connected.

The nice lady put a puppy in the girl's arms. Again she said "We came here to see these guys", and the man said, "No, we came here for him", as he was still looking at me. The girl looked at me and said "Oh my GOD he is adorable", and in the next breath, "What do you think of this little guy?" referring to the puppy in her arms. She plopped it into the man's arms.

The nice lady said "This is Eddie", looking at me. By then I remembered about the strong cute dogs getting adopted.

So I started barking and doing zoomies up and down the kennel. The man continued to stare and smiled at me. The girl did too. She said, "So you don't want a puppy" and the man said, "No, I think Eddie is why we are here."

CHAPTER 2

BOBBY AND TRACY

The nice lady grabbed a leash and opened my kennel. She put the leash on me and introduced me to Bobby and Tracy. Bobby looked at Tracy and said, "Don't you agree? We are here for Eddie?" I did my best to be the cutest I could be. I looked at her and let her rub on me while leaning into her. It was as if something or some being crawled inside of me and made me behave this way.

It was as if I was fearless. My tummy ache was gone, and I was a different dog. I was not me. I was watching myself behaving like this and was amazed. "What a good actor", I thought to myself.

The nice lady said his owner had to leave him behind. There was some more talk, but I could not understand. Bobby gave Tracy a hug and kiss and said, "See you and Eddie at home, I am hungry." Off he went and there I was on the leash with Tracy. She filled out some paperwork and out the door I went with her. She opened the back of her car and invited me in, so up I hopped.

We made a stop and Tracy left me in the car in the parking lot as she went into the building.

Suddenly life came into the NOW! I'm back!

I am wondering if I am going to another kennel.

As I sit there wondering what's going to happen, Tracy opens the car door and says, "Look, I got you a new bed!"

We drive to Tracy and Bobby's home and Bobby greets me when I get out of the car. They show me around the house. I like the warm and loving smells I am smelling.

Just when I am getting some good sniffs in, Tracy encourages me into the bathroom and the next thing I know, I am in their tub being scrubbed. Water is not a favorite thing of mine, and I am feeling a bit odd.

Tracy says, we have to get the stink off of you. I have grown to like my new smell, but she insists that she scrub it off.

She towel-dries me and snuggles me. I like her feel and allow her to keep snuggling on me although it is a bit much and I would like to get back to exploring some new sniffs with my new clean smell.

CHAPTER 3

TRUST

I awake to being kissed and hearing "Good morning little man"....Where the heck? What the ....I am clueless about where I am. I am laying on the carpet next to Papa and Tracy's bed being rubbed and kissed. It reminds me of what happened yesterday. I am so comfortable.

"Come on Eddie, let's go potty", she says. Really, urghhhh, she does not know that I can hold it forever. Why must I remove myself from this amazing position to go 'potty' right now? "Potty, come on Eddie Bear." I follow her to the door and she opens it to a cold burst and encourages me out.

I give her my best pleading look, "Don't make me."

"Out Eddie, go potty!" Out I walk with my head hanging low. Oh, the morning chill hits me. And I am walking down the stairs of the deck to 'potty'. There are amazing smells in this yard, my nose is not the best and still, I can smell the goodness. I do my business and stop smelling to hurry back into the warmth of the home.

Tracy and Papa are scurrying about....actually Tracy is, Papa has this energy about him that is light. He moves slow and steady with no urgency. Tracy's energy is different. She is fast and heavy on her feet. She is not a big person, maybe 5'3 and small…although I get the feeling she thinks she is big. They weave in and out of each other methodically. "What should we do with him?" Tracy says. "Leave him in the kennel or not? I am just not sure."

Bobby is thinking and getting my breakfast. "Here you go Eddie, some food for you my friend, and down comes the shiny bowl with my food. It was filled up! Wow! I feel special! Both Papa and Tracy keep talking to me as if I was a human. "What do you think Eddie, Papa says? Are you ok outside of the kennel?"

I wish I could tell them yes. I have never been one to 'wreck' furniture. Although I don't know why they are asking me this.

As they moved about there was a warmness to their 'morning hustle.' They speak to each other in calm voices. I feel their calmness wash over me as I eat some breakfast.

They are both dressed now, and Tracy asks me politely to get in my kennel, which I oblige. Tracy kisses me several times and she tells me that I am home. She says, "We love you, Eddie." How could she say that to me? I am a bad boy. She may say that after one night, but………….still I must not trust her.

Papa says, Eddie, "We are going to work and will be home very soon. We are not sure if you need to be in the kennel but we want you to feel safe, so for now this is the best place. We will be home very soon, do not worry."

The kennel door closes and they continue talking about me and their day. They hug and kiss each other and then the house door shuts. They are gone.

Hmmmffff....now what? I wondered, should I try to break out of here? I could dig, but I don't think I could through the heavy metal door or plastic that surrounds me. As my thoughts whirl about, something, someone was there with me. I was frightened at first and then I wasn't. Whatever being it was, was very close. Hello?! Hello?! Please don't hurt me. Hello?! Please who are you? This being is right next to me in the kennel!!!! I cannot see or feel it, but I know it's right there, standing right next to me in the kennel.

I want to bark, and then....then....then.....a wave of light comes over me. The room is filled up with bright, warm light. It's all around me. It seems to be on me and seems even inside of me. I feel this warmth like I had never felt before.

I am unable to speak and not afraid. I am ok. Whatever this being is it's kind and loving and letting me know that I'm ok and that my future is going to be ok.

What is that noise? It is a door, I bark and hear her voice, "Hi Eddie, it's me, I am home." I had been sound asleep, so sound I did not know where I was or who the familiar voice greeting me was. I shake my head. Wait, where am I? Who is this person that speaks my name as if she has known me forever?

There is her face, Tracy! Ahhhh ...yes, it came back to me. I am in Tracy and Bobby's home. The kennel door opens, and she asks me how I did? She speaks to me as if we were old friends. She invites me outside. So out I go to sniff and 'potty'. She comes outside with me. She's chatting away telling me about the neighbors and looking around to see if any of them are out. It is winter and cold out. We were only out a short time and back in the house. Still, she chats away. She tells me where she was and what she did for a living. None of it makes much sense, although I do get the feeling that she is able to come and go as she pleases. It seemed like she was not gone that long, however, I could be wrong. I'm still so tired.

Tracy encourages me to rest. She has a business where she works often from home and I hear her on the phone throughout the rest of the day as I ease in and out of gentle slumber.

I feel a tenseness in her voice at times on the phone and her body language telling me that she is not happy. Then there were times when she's on the phone and her whole body and voice are different. They are soft. I am unsure of why sometimes she seems so tense and other times soft. I enjoy the new sniffs and the warm, loving 'being' returned off and on reminding me that I am safe. It also fills my heart with something…the only word that comes to me is love, however, I was trying my best to block it. I knew love once or twice and it hurt badly. I did not want to feel that hurt ever again, so when the 'being' tries to fill up my heart, I block it.

This is what I remember about those days…

Here's how it was…Bobby came home sometime in the evening and Tracy had prepared dinner. I got to eat out of my new shiny bowl and it was kept full for me. I ate what I wanted and left the rest for later. It felt different to leave some. I trusted that they would not take it away from me as others had done. I am not sure where this trust was coming from, but I trusted, and my bowl remained filled with food.

Tracy and Bobby sat at the dining table eating, talking, and laughing. They talked about their day and often about ME! I liked that. After dinner, they put on warm clothes and jackets and put a collar on me. They had taken my collar off when I came into their home last night. It felt nice to not have something around my neck.

I was unsure of what was happening, and they could see the fear in my eyes. They told me, "It is ok Eddie, we are going for a walk." They put me on a leash and we walked outside as one big pack.

There was a whole new world outside their house. We were greeted by people living across the street. I was introduced to them as if I was a person. They were very kind and had two little humans. I was not allowed close to them which saddened me. I wanted to sniff them. We quickly moved down the street.

I loved smelling all the new 'pee mail' from the other dogs in the neighborhood. There was so much to smell. We continued to a school with woods and a large field. Tracy wanted me off the leash, Bobby was cautious. He asked me if I would run away.

I had run away once.

I was living with my first family, and they were angry and loud. The man hit me often telling me how bad I was. I got away once and ran fast....oh so very fast! It seems like another lifetime ago, but I remember being on the street and running so fast. I was captured by someone and put in their car. They returned me to the angry people. I was sad, but I knew I had a job there to protect the little human baby. I did my best.

I quickly remembered where I was and realized the leash was off me. I was FREE! Oh......I ran and sniffed. Tracy and Bobby watched me and stayed close to me. There was something ..... well ..... magical about them. Again, they were talking and laughing and holding hands. As they did this, they included me in their conversations. Often Tracy reached down to touch me and tell me nice things. She said "Thank you, Eddie, thank you Eddie for choosing us." She had said this many times over the last 24 hours. When she said it, her eyes filled up with tears.

I felt fun and light freedom as I ran and sniffed and watched Tracy and Bobby. They laughed, played, and chatted with me as if we had been together all our lives. I wanted this moment to never end. I was introduced to several people at the school and neighbors on the way back to the house.

Back in the house, it was warm and toasty and well...well...it felt like home. How could this be that I felt so at home in just 24 hours? How could I feel so much love and yet try to hold back that feeling? I was trying to be strong and cautious and not love too much. I knew too well what happened when I let my guard down. I needed to remain of the mindset that "I can be thrown out at any moment."

As this thought entered and played with my mind, Tracy said, "Hey Eddie...come here!" She was sitting on their bed..."Come on Eddie, come here!" I headed for the bedroom and looked at Papa as if to say "Well?"

Papa looked down at me. "Come on up Eddie." I hopped up.

To my surprise, Tracy snuggled me as I had never been snuggled. My resolve melted away..I was thinking "It is so warm and comfy and loving up here! Ohhhh"... Tracy was rubbing my tummy, my neck and kissing me....kissing and kissing and more kisses. More thoughts come..."I feel loved right this second! She certainly is a kisser."

"Oh, Eddie you are a good boy, and soft and sweet, and so cuddly!" she cooed.

Again, thinking "I must be in heaven...or somewhere that is not real....this is amazing! I never want this feeling to stop!"

I remember falling asleep in Tracy's arms and waking once to Papa crawling in and scratching me. "You are a good boy", he whispered.

Memories...I want to live them again.

I know...It's easier for me to talk in the now, it makes the memories more real. I'll do that.

I am aware of his generosity and gratitude.

I feel a connection to this guy that I have never known, and I like it. Sometime in the night, I wake, I feel hot. I also still feel love. I am thirsty so I hop down and head to my bowl filled with fresh water.

I don't like yucky old water or hitting my tongue on the bottom of the bowl, so I appreciate the full clean bowl of water. I think I will sleep in my kennel, once I arrange the blankets in it so they are just right. I have to have them fixed to hold my head up. It takes me a bit of adjusting to get settled in and then…there it is ….again it is with me. The presence of the being is next to me in the kennel. It is communicating to me that I am loved. Who are you? Where are you? I want to see you. I get nothing but warmth all over my body. I have questions and I find my eyes closing…I can't communicate anymore. I am very comfy and sleepy now.

CHAPTER 4

SMELLS AND SAND

It has been one week since I have been living with Papa and Tracy. I have already been on many adventures. Today they are taking me for a ride and telling me that the place we are going to is amazing. I am excited and can barely stand my excitement in the car. I can't hold back as I whimper excitedly. Ohhhh how I love to roam free and explore all sorts of new 'pee mail'.

We only drive for a few minutes and pull into a parking area. I let out a whimper of excitement as again I can't contain it! Tracy is giggling. "Hold on Eddie ...almost there!"

We park and my door is opened! We are here Eddie! Come on Papa, let me show you this amazing place, says Tracy! Papa calls her Momma to me. So I am starting to think her name is Momma rather than Tracy.

Oh, the smells are good here! Lots of pee-mail. Some smells I can't make out. My nose is not the sharpest.

We are winding through the woods and come to a path that runs along a fence. Loud noises are buzzing around inside the fence. I am not sure what they are but they are moving fast and very loud. People are on things with 2 wheels moving fast, flying over sand dunes. Up and down they go. Papa seems annoyed by the noise. "This is your spot Momma?"

Wow…sooooo loud. "Well, it is quiet during the week", she says. I don't care, I like it! As we walk along Momma and Papa talk, she giggles often. Sometimes they stop and kiss. My heart flutters.

What the…….!!!!! I am looking at the largest sand dune I have ever seen! "Come on guys!" Mom shouts and runs ahead of us! Up the hill, she runs! I am determined to catch her! Papa runs with me! What a sight to see! The little 2 wheeled buzzers are buzzing around a course below us. We can see for miles! There are mountains and ocean, and oh the air is so fresh up here!

"I want to show you the cliff", Mom says. We follow her, Papa and me. We come to the edge of the dune and look down at a beach/ocean. It is very steep and very high up. I feel like anything is possible right now! I love this feeling and I don't want to ever leave here! A chill runs through me and I remember it is cold out. Papa is cold now too as there is a little wind blowing.

"Come on", he says, "Eddie and I are cold." It is as if he can read my mind.

"Oh ok, party poopers", she says…and back we walk. Papa's car feels so nice and warm. I have blankets in the back seat. When Papa takes me for rides without Mom, I get to sit upfront in the seat next to him. Today, I rode in the back.

As we are driving home, Mom's phone rings. Her voice and body change as she talks. She seems stressed and frustrated. Once off the phone, she talks to Papa about the call. I can't figure out what happened, but there is a shift in her personality. I hope I didn't do anything wrong. I feel concerned. We ride home in silence. I am confused. What just happened.

Once home Mom heads for the shower. Papa looks down at me...."It is ok, Eddie, Mom has to go to work. You and I are going to hang out, ok?" Again, I am a bit confused.

Mom gets dressed and does her hair. She is bustling about quickly. She is ignoring me and Papa. She is on a mission, and I try to stay out of her way.

She grabs her keys and bag, kisses Papa, and bends down to me. "Eddie, I love you, I will be back soon." Off she goes.

I stare at the door that closes behind her. Hmmmffff..... I feel Papa's eyes on me and turn around. " It is ok Eddie, she gets stressed sometimes. She is going to work now. She will be showing some people their new home. She is coming back soon. Let's hang out. Do you want to go run errands with me?" I like the word GO and don't understand much else of what he said, so I wag my tail and do a little happy dance.

Papa grabs his keys and coat and off we GO!

The afternoon was a blur as I fell asleep. We stopped many times and Papa got out of the car. He always turns the car on when he is gone long and it was warm and toasty inside. I feel safe with him. I like GOING with him.

After several stops and GOs, we are pulling back into the garage. Mom's car is in the garage and I get excited to see her. She is home Eddie, Papa says…I told you she would come home!

Inside we go. Eddie!!!! Mom yells from the kitchen. I run to her for scratches and kisses. Have I told you, she loves to kiss me! The kitchen smells of good smells and she is smiling again. All feels right with the world.

CHAPTER 5

MYSTERIOUS WOODS AND THE MOOSE ENCOUNTER

I am enjoying my new life and feeling more and more at home each day. I still hold back from full-on "letting go" and letting Mom and Papa see the "real me". I am hesitant as I don't want to be given away again. I am not sure my heart could live through it again.

I give what I can and enjoy each day that I get to be in their home.

Most days, I get to go somewhere for exercise, and I have met lots of nice people and pups. My favorite place to go is the Dog Park five minutes down the street. Tons of great sniffs.

Papa goes to work early and comes home late, Mom is in and out, and I can't figure out her schedule. She seems to do her own thing, however, oftentimes she switches into a stressed-out soul. I dislike when that happens to her and try my best to be a good boy during those times. I get afraid when she is not happy.

We have lots of snow on the ground today. Papa says, "Hey Eddie, want to go for a walk to the school?" I love going with him, so I wag my tail, whimper, and jump up and down. When I hear him say GO this happens to my body.

My collar gets put on and off we go. We are walking to what is starting to feel familiar - the school. I like the school. Good sniffs and close to home. Come on Eddie, let's go into the woods. The woods are filled with mystery. I smell pee-mail and other smells from non-pups. I can go fast on the groomed trails. Today there is much snow, and it is deep so I am unable to move quickly.

I turn off the trail into the deep snow as I smell something interesting. It has my curiosity. Ohhhh NOOOO!!! What is happening? Papa yells "EDDIE!!!! COME! EDDIE! COME!" I can't move, I am stuck in the snow.

NO ….She is hissing at me! OH NO! Her hooves are on my shoulder blades. Papa! Papa! HELP ME! HELP ME! Papa is screaming at her - she turns and runs. I can't move, I hurt!

I don't want Papa to be mad at me. I feel like I am losing consciousness …what happened? I hear him talking. He is trying to pick me up. "Can you walk Eddie? Can you move?"

I try walking….it hurts Papa-it hurts bad! Again he tries to lift me. Ouch! I hurt. I am trying not to whimper but I hurt so bad. He is walking. I know I am heavy. "Come on Eddie-try walking. We are almost to Mom." I am unsure where I am walking - I am very foggy. It seems to take forever to get wherever we are going.

Then I hear a door, we are in Mom's car. Papa is wrapping me with a blanket. "DRIVE! Drive Tracy! A Moose stomped his back. He got stuck in the snow and couldn't move."

"Eddie, I got you. You are ok. We love you", she says from the front.

I am floating in and out, and then awake inside the doctor's office. I am in so much pain.

They ask to take x-rays of my body and Papa says yes. He retells the whole story although I don't remember it. I remember to GO. I like to GO. I like to Go with Papa.

They give me something - urghhhh...I hate medicine. Yuk! I am being prodded and probed everywhere. I want to go home. I want to cry, I hurt everywhere.

We are heading home, and I feel tingly and numbness setting in. I am so sleepy.

I awake to treats and being wrapped in warm blankets. Mom, Papa, and Uncle Dave are in the room. Mom is rubbing my back. I hurt so badly. I vaguely remember a monster stepping on my back. It was awful.

I am being pampered and so loved by Mom and Papa. I feel an amazing sense of being taken care of. In my other homes, I felt the need to care for the humans. I never felt like anyone noticed if I didn't feel good. Today, I am being noticed and I sorta like it!

I am falling in and out of sleep. Mom keeps bringing warm blankets and I am sinking into them. My bones ache. Every so often I am told to eat something and after I eat the yummy treat, I feel sleepy and more relaxed.

Mom encourages me to get up and go potty. She has this thing about me peeing every few hours. She has yet to learn that I can hold it forever. Oh well….because I don't want to upset her, I will pee. Oh, ouch, it hurts to move. Down the stairs, I go. Out into the cold. I feel cold out here. My brain hurts and I feel fuzzy. I am doing my business and walking quickly back up the stairs …I want to sleep.

Into the house, Papa says "Eddie, you want some supper? You haven't eaten anything." I am so sleepy. I walk to my bowl and sniff….oh I am so sleepy. I want my bed. I want today to end. I crawl into my kennel and Mom quickly puts the nice warm blankets around me. I don't remember much…I know I woke a few times to Mom wanting me to pee and Papa saying leave him to sleep. I sleep.

I wake to terrible pain. I want to cry and be held. What happened ….I quickly remember the monster coming down with her hooves on my back. I flinch! Maybe if I fall back to sleep I will wake and it will all be a bad dream. I can't go back to sleep. I am so thirsty. I walk out of the kennel to my water bowl, then remember..oh yeah, I forgot to eat dinner, and I am a bit hungry. I munch a few kibbles. Then head into Mom and Papa's room. Mom awakes to me staring up at her.

"Eddie my boy"….out of the bed to her knees. She hugs me and it hurts. I know she wants to love me, but I'm hurt. I let her know it hurts by pulling away. "Do you want to snuggle in with us

Eddie?" I give her my brown eye stare - yes. She helps me up into their very high bed. Ouch!!!! I hurt Mom! She wraps me gently and is careful to not hurt me, crawling in next to me.

Papa is awake too and scratches my head…."We love you Eddie….so sorry you hurt. We are here and we love you." I fall soundly back to sleep until they both awake for work.

I hear them talking about their day and then Mom appears. "Eddie, you have to go pee and eat some breakfast ok?" I don't want to move. Maybe if I pretend she is not there, she will leave me alone. I will lay here very still and pretend I don't hear her. "Eddie"…..she is looking at me hmffffff…… I open one eye to her an inch from my face. "Ohhhhh Eddie, I am so sorry you hurt. Come on get up and pee and eat something. I want to get another pain pill in you, and you need food."

Urghhhhhh……..go away my eyes are trying to tell her.

She nudges me. Ohhhhhhh…..ghessshhhhh……I stand and try to stretch but I hurt. "Bobby", Mom says …come here…Papa rushes in.

"What?"

"Look." Mom is pointing to my back. "Look…poor Eddie!" Papa touches where she is pointing and it is like little needles are on my back. I flinch. "Oh Eddie", he says, "I am sorry. Come on buddy, let's get another pain pill in you." He lifts me so gently off the bed. His touch is always so gentle and kind.

Papa feeds me chicken and it tastes so good. I have some breakfast and slowly carefully walk outside to do my business. I usually sniff around a bit, but I am quick to get my business done and get back into the house. I am starting to feel relaxed and sleepy again.

Into the warm house and my kennel again. Mom wraps me up. I fade out and hear the door shutting and Mom saying goodbye Eddie we love you and will be home soon. Click. Drifting to sleep.....sleep feels so good. I am so relaxed.

CHAPTER 6

THE HEALER

I am feeling much better although I am carrying a big 'sack' on my back. It feels warm, heavy, and often itches. Mom is concerned. Dad mentions a lady named Clarissa. I am not sure what they are chatting about, however, a lady named Clarissa appears today.

She is very nice and soft-spoken. She has strong hands and sits on our floor in the living room. I am not certain what she and Mom are chatting about, however, I do know that I am the center of their conversation.

Clarissa puts her hands on me. I like the feel …she is not pushing or pulling me rather guiding me with her hands. Mom is watching carefully and Clarissa shows her a few things to do on my body using her hands. Ohhhhh….I like the feeling. I think I will sit down and let her keep doing this. Mom puts her hands on me too. Mom can be a bit….well …rough. She stops and lets Clarissa touch me. I am feeling amazing and then my back starts tingling. I move away from both of them. I am not certain I am feeling good anymore. They go about chatting a while longer and Clarissa leaves.

Mom starts bustling about as usual. I often follow her up and down the stairs and throughout the house. Tonight, I go lay down in our bedroom.

"Eddie, are you ok? Come here and give me hugs"…says, Mom. I have recently started displaying my affections towards Mom by 'hugging' her. She seems to like this little move I have created….so I do it from time to time. I keep my back legs on the floor as she kneels on the floor, and lift my front legs up, one paw on each side of her neck. Mom makes this funny little giggle noise and loves on me. "Oh Eddie, I love you to pieces and pieces of pie, way up in the sky." Her arms wrap tightly around me and she gives me a little squeeze.

What the?!!!! The lump on my back makes an odd feeling and moves in her arms like a lump of clay mixed with water. She quickly puts me down and touches my lump. It feels funny and also I feel relief for the first time since that moose landed on my back.

I am too excited and want to share my excitement with 'zoomiessss' all over the house! "Eddddddie!!!! Eddie!," Mom giggles!

With that Papa walks in the front door. Quickly I race down the stairs to share the news and excitement with him!!! Mom is beaming at him and quickly tells him of Clarissa's visit and our special hug! "The lump just dispersed", she says smiling!

We all do happy dances and I wag my tail uncontrollably! I fell in love a little more today with Papa and Momma.

CHAPTER 7

DOG PARK CHATTER

Each day seems to be filled with love and adventures! Most days I get to go meet new pups and their humans at this fun place Mom and Papa call the Dog Park! This place is filled with amazing 'pee mail' that tells stories of all the pups that visit. I love sniffing and learning about them through their pee-mail! So many of them leave important messages about their lives. I often respond by peeing over their pee message with hopes that the pup will get my message. We have so much to say to each other and this is my one shot each day to sniff and connect to my own kind.

Mom often chit chats and walks with other humans. Sometimes I get antsy as she stops for a long time chatting. Papa does not chat. He is on a mission to walk. Although we stroll so I can get the maximum amount of sniff time. When Mom and she are not chatting, we are fast walking. Sometimes she runs. I prefer walking and slowing it down, however, I am happy to be in this land of magic smells, so I take what I can get.

CHAPTER 8

THE COMMUNICATOR

One evening Mom and Papa are both home and Mom is busily cleaning up the house. This is often an indication of a visitor. I am curious. Sure enough, the doorbell rings, and I do my best to protect our home. I have a very big bark and frighten humans until they see me...then for some reason, they seem to smile at me. Or say things like, "'Wow, you are smaller than I had imagined!" I may be small, but I pack a mean bark and can defend our home from unwanted beings!

The door opens to a lovely human they call, Lee. I feel as if we have met before. She has a soothing voice and way about her. She enters and talks to Mom and Papa for a while before sitting at our dining table. She is opening her pack and pulling out a pen and notebook. Mom and Papa are sitting on the couch and loveseat listening to Lee. I am getting an odd feeling.

The next thing I know Lee is speaking to me!!! Yes, speaking my language! I can understand everything she is saying to me!!! I am over the moon excited and at the same time apprehensive and a little cautious. I have never had this sort of communication with a human and it is a peculiar feeling. Lee first asked permission to communicate with me, I hesitated and then agreed to communicate.

This is how it went: Lee asked me, "Eddie, is there anything that you would like to tell me?

Me: "Yes, am I able to share with you now, this is my first time talking like this to a human. I do like it here. This is a nice and good place. I like it here. There is another one that lives here. She is a loved dog and I feel her here often. She keeps me company, even though I can't see her. She is helping me to feel at home here and she welcomes me. She tells me all about Tracy and Bobby.

Lee: "Oh this is wonderful, Eddie. Does that help you, hearing from Orca Jean?"

Me: "Yes! Yes, she makes me feel that I can maybe trust again."

Lee, "Is it hard for you to trust?"

Me, "Yes, I am trying to not let my heart close off and make sure that my heart stays open. Orca Jean is helping me with this. She is a warm and gentle light that is helping my heart to stay open to trust."

Lee: "Can you tell me more about this, Eddie?"

Me: "It is hard now for me to love so freely. I have loved before. I had many in my life, many little ones in my life that I loved so much. They were my family, and I was their "special boy" but I don't know what happened. Was I a bad boy? I am so sad."

Lee: "No, Eddie. You were never a bad boy. You are a beautiful and wonderful special boy. Your family before could not take you with them. This broke their hearts. They love you so very much but could not take you with them."

Me: "I thought we would always be together. Why did they leave me like that?"

Lee: "The man had to go far away and he had to move his family far away. He could not take you because he had to go far away."

Me, "Couldn't I have gone with him? Why?"

Lee: "No, Eddie. He could not take you with him and this made him very sad."

Me: "I still feel him. I still feel his sadness and his love."

Lee: "Is this hard for you, to feel his sadness and his love?

Lee stops writing, she puts her pen down and cries. She feels my pain and sadness internally. Bobby and Tracy get very concerned, and remain quiet.

Me: "Yes and no. It helps me to stay connected to him...to all of them. I miss them. This makes me sad sometimes but not as much as it used to."

Lee: "I am glad to hear this, Eddie. Is there anything else you want to share?"

Me: "This is so hard and here goes. The little one....the youngest one, does she miss me? I can still feel her. Please, will you please tell her that I love her?"

Lee: "I am not able to tell her for you because I do not know her but I would think that this child will always love and remember you."

Me: "This makes me happy to be so loved."

Lee: "Eddie, your first family that you lived with tried to find you, too. They wanted you to come back and live with them."

Me: "Oh! I am happy that I did not go back there. There was a lot of anger and yelling in that house. I was sometimes afraid there and am glad not to be there. I did love the little ones."

Lee: "Thank you, Eddie for telling me. I will tell Bobby and Tracy for you. Are you feeling o.k. here and are you getting less sad?"

She sure was helping me to feel better. "Yes, this is a good and wonderful place, and I am safe here. I know that I am loved here, and I know that this is a good dog house. I know that they too lost love and she is still close by for them. I know this is a home where I can grow old, right?"

Lee: "yes, Eddie, you can grow old here. This is your forever home and Tracy and Bobby are your forever humans."

I am so relieved. "This is so good to know as I chose them and waited for them, hoping they would come. Are there young ones here? Do young ones come to visit?"

Lee: "Tracy says that there is a young one who comes to stay here every other month. Would you like that?"

Me: "Oh, yes! I like young ones if they are not too quick to move or too loud. That makes me nervous, and I feel like I need to have order."

Lee: "I will tell this to Tracy and Bobby for you. Eddie, Tracy would like me to ask you if are you aggressive toward other dogs? She wonders if you want to hurt or dominate other dogs?"

Me: "No, not really. I like to play and run mostly but if another dog comes too close to my nose, I get nervous."

Lee: "What makes you nervous when a dog comes too close to your nose?"

Me: "I don't seem to smell as clearly as I used to, so sometimes I might misunderstand a smell."

Lee: "I will tell Bobby and Tracy for you."

Me: "Thank you. I am feeling very fine and very calm. All seems well and safe."

Lee: "I will tell them for you, Eddie. Is there anything else that you would like to share with me to tell Tracy and Bobby?

I feel like I have so much to say and so I tell this nice lady, "Yes. Sometimes I get fearful about having to go away again and I hide my fear. So sometimes my stomach hurts but I hide this, too. This is when I might get more aggressive with another dog, when my stomach hurts."

Lee: "Oh, Eddie, I will tell Tracy and Bobby for you. What will help you relax a bit more?"

Me: "I would like reassurance, a lot of reassurance. If they can tell me that they are here forever and that I can grow old here. I want to grow old here. This is important for me to hear. Even when my hips hurt and I'm old, I want to grow old here."

Lee: "Eddie, Tracy and Bobby are telling me to tell you that they want you to grow old here. They love you."

Me: "Oh, this is wonderful. I am pleased."

Lee: "I am glad this pleases you. You are a wonderful and special boy. Bobby would like me to ask you what do you like to do?"

Bobby is Papa and I am so glad he asked me this question! "I love to jump for the ball. I love to walk and run. I love to snuggle under the covers. I love to lead when I walk. I love to be a lead dog. I love to ride in the car. I love the wind. I love the grass, but it makes me sneeze. I love the smells of food cooking. I love to be held. I love soft arms around me. I love sighs. I love soft voices. These humans have everything I want. Please tell them, they are warm, gentle and kind. Oh, please tell them that I would like to go with them to their office, I want to go to work and be a greeter and a welcomer. I like to see new people and people I know. It is so nice to see kind eyes. I like to have a job, to take care of things. To keep things in order

I also like feeling calm and happy. I like being with Orca Jean and feeling her presence close to me. I like bubbles. I like to play with hats like I did with my other family."

Lee: "Thank you, Eddie. I will tell Tracy and Bobby for you. Is there anything else?"

Me: "Yes, it will take some time for me to let them totally get to know me. I am a little more funny than I am being right now."

Lee, "I will tell them for you. Bobby would like to know if you are allergic to anything?"

Papa wants to know all about me. "Yes, I am allergic to dust, grass and corn."

Lee: "Thank you, Eddie. I will tell them for you. Tracy has told me to tell you that you have brought a lot of laughter and love to them and to their home, and Bobby says that when you're an older dog, if your hips hurt you, they will take care of you and do whatever they can to love you and make you feel safe and happy."

Me: "This brings me peace, wonderful peace. I am grateful. My pain and sadness has been very big and deep and I can totally trust now."

Lee: "Yes, darling Eddie. You can totally trust this family. Tracy and Bobby will be your forever humans."

Me: "I am so appreciative to you. I think I will be able to breathe well and completely again. Thank you."

Lee: "Thank you, Eddie. Thank you for talking with me. Blessings to you, dearest heart. Beautiful, sweet Eddie. Thank you for talking with me and for sharing your beautiful heart. You are a **special boy**."

Me: "You are welcome. Thank you, will you come here again?"

Lee: "Yes, Eddie. Thank you, dear one. Blessings to you."

And I felt so much relief and goodness and the communicator left. I was a new dog and excited to share my real self with Tracy and Bobby, Momma and Papa!

CHAPTER 9

NEW AND FUN ENERGY

Now that Papa and Momma know my 'needs' as communicated via Lee, I anticipate some new activities in my life. My mood seems lighter and there is a weight off of my mind and my soul. It seems that I can now LOVE with my whole soul. I can let the humans see who I am, all of me. The energy in our home is exciting and fun!

Mom and Papa are snuggled in for the night watching a movie. I am snuggled in between them, my favorite place to be. Papa gets up to get a snack and I am hopeful he remembers to bring me one too. Mom gets up to do something and I slide off the soft leather sofa to watch Papa in the kitchen. The afghan falls upon me and I am trapped. Here I sit, waiting for them to return. I can see out the holes, so I wait patiently. They both come back at the same time and snuggle back into their spots on the sofa not even noticing that ....ummm...hello, I am missing guys!

Then Papa sees me and starts laughing hysterically, he points and Mom starts laughing.

I continue to sit blinking through the holes of the afghan at them. My tail is wagging as I watch the two of them. Mom is snorting and she is laughing so hard. Papa falls to the floor.....I continue peering out blinking at them. Ahhhh yes, I am funny and I am finally able to show them just how funny I can be! This is my true self. They finally contain themselves although Mom runs to the bathroom! I ask for help getting out of this crazy position stuck under the afghan and Papa helps me! We are connected on a deeper level. This makes my soul sing!

CHAPTER 10

CELEBRITY STATUS

Most days I get to go to the Dog Park which is down the street from our home. When I go with Papa, we weave in and out of people, there is no hurry and no need for chit-chat. This does not mean Papa is rude. He, like me, keeps his thoughts and much of his voice to himself. He is friendly, kind and above all courteous with others…a true gentleman. He does not need to make new friends or impress others. We walk at a nice pace allowing me to catch up on all my pee-mail.

This is my time to review or sniff pee. I learn so much from the other K9s by reading (sniffing) their scent. So many of them are in fear, unhappy, have upset tummies, or are simply filled with love and life! I love all the scents at the park.

Now when I go with Mom, it is a different story. She tells Papa when walking together that he is 'lala gagging' ….I am not sure what that means. I know Papa does not appreciate it. Mom moves fast and encourages me to move fast, which means less sniff time. I love sniffing and don't like to power walk, but I love her, so I keep up.

Mom also likes to chat with others. She often stops and chats for a while with them. I don't like to walk fast and I also don't like to stop and chat for long periods.

She can chat! Conversations range from what 'type' of dog I am, to her work, their work, and Mom asks lots of questions. Sometimes we continue walking with these strangers.

One of my communication wishes via Lee came true today! I was not sure what was up as Mom was using different words. She told me I was needed at her office, and I was unsure what that meant. I was happy to go with her when she told me to get in the car. I love being with either one of the humans and especially riding in the car.

Off we go. Not sure where, but I am eager about where we are heading. We are pulling up in front of a building and many cars and several people are bustling about. 'Wait, Eddie,' Mom says. She is clipping my leash to my collar, and I become aware of many new sniffs. 'Come on, we get to go to work,' she says. I am following along as we enter the building. Mom is greeting others and they smile at me. Some ask the proverbial question, "What is he'?" I mostly ignore this, I am a family member ghessssshhhhhh. They ask that question as if I can't hear them.

What …wait….what is this? "Come on Eddie, get in", she says. Two ginormous doors have opened, and it seems to be a sort of box that is suspended in the air. I enter as I want to please 'her' but it does not feel stable under my feet. The doors slam shut and there is a loud beep. We are moving. This is a peculiar feeling. I am not sure if I like it or what I am feeling. Boom, we stop and the doors open. I follow her lead.

She puts her key in a door and we walk. We walk around a hall and then enter another hall. I wish she would slow down so I could sniff my surroundings. There is so much to sniff. She puts her key in another door and we walk into a small rectangular box-like space. It smells like her. She tells me to lay down and relax. She is taking her coat off and sits down in front of the box-like thing that she spends hours staring at daily. Hmmmffff......that's it, lay down, relax? Doesn't she remember, I like to greet people?

It seems like I have been laying here, "relaxing" forever, and then I hear movement in the hallway. Woof! Woof! 'Eddie, NO...no bark! She says. I want to protect her at all times, so I continue woof...just a tad quieter. Who is that? A man enters the room and kneels down to me. "Well hello, you must be Eddie?" he says. Mom introduces me officially to her office neighbor, Tom. He smells nice, I think I like him. I walk out into the hallway to catch some more smells. "Eddie", Mom says, "come back in here." Ghessshhhhh! Ok, ok. Back into the office I go. Tom leaves and the door shuts. I am trying to relax and lay down again. I am dozing off and someone else enters her office.

"Ohhhhhhhh......who are you?" She says to me. I'm excited. I feel honored to greet her. What a lovely soul this Patty is. She tells me how handsome I am and what a good boy I am.

Mom says, "Pat gave me the yummy gift last week and the sock toy." I like her.

What a fun day we had at Mom's office. I am told throughout the day what a wonderful boy I am, petted, scratched and hear the occasional "What is he?. I love working with Mom. We arrive home and I am exhausted. Mom goes about chores in the house, and I go snuggle in and rest. I dream of all the nice people and smells I experienced today.

As the week moves forward, I get multiple jobs. Work with Mom and going to homes where Mom is meeting people and a photographer to take photos of the homes. I am asked to stand, sit, walk and wait often. The nice photographer snaps photos of me in many different locations of several homes. I am told that I am a celebrity and will be helping homeowners sell their homes. I love the attention and all the new sniffs. It is fun meeting all these nice people and being a part of Mom's business. I feel important, needed, and loved.

CHAPTER 11

LITTLE PEOPLE AND LAUGHTER

Tonight, Papa and I head to the dog park or as Papa calls it, the DP. We are moving along at our comfortable pace, Papa allowing me to sniff all the new sniffs and a little boy and girl approach us. The little girl points at my head and loudly proclaims, "Look at his head, it is HUGE!"

The little boy that is with her quickly responds, "He must be a very smart dog because of his head size." I like him and I approach his little body for a quick scratch and then we move along.

Little people are interesting to me, and I will always be on the lookout for the little people that I used to live with. I hope to someday run into them and tell them how much I love them.

We stroll through the park, saying hi to many of our friends that we see here, and there are new faces and puppies too. The new puppies want to jump on me. I nudge them with my big chest letting them know some basic dog etiquette. I let them know that jumping will get you in trouble, but sniffing is ok. Their humans like that I am a gentle trainer, and they encourage me to help their young pups.

We return home to Momma just pulling in the driveway. I am excited to see her and wish she would have been with us at the DP. She would have loved seeing me teaching the young ones and I love when we are all together.

Papa grabs her and gives her a big hug and tells her about the little boy and girl. He smiles when sharing about the little boy saying how smart I am because of my head. I am beaming. I like when Papa speaks about me.

We are all in the house and Momma and Papa are sitting in the living room. I head to my water bowl and suddenly hear laughter and then silence and more laughter. Papa says, "Listen to our little man, he is drinking rhythmically." They giggle some more as I continue to drink.

Momma says, "One, two, three, pause, one, two, three." She is saying the numbers in sync with my licks into my water bowl. This is the way I have always drunk water and I am not sure why it amuses them so. I do love to hear them laugh, so I continue to drink a little longer than my thirst just to entertain the humans.

CHAPTER 12

MOUNTAINS AND GRANDPARENTS

Momma is moving fast today. She is zipping around the house cleaning 3 different rooms at the same time. I try to keep up with her and her pace exhausts me, so I lay in a spot that I am able to keep my eyes on, or sort of. Papa tells me when he leaves the house that it is my job to protect Momma, a job I take seriously, but when she moves this fast it is hard. She seems tense and is talking to herself. Something is up and I am concerned.

Papa arrives home and Momma is short-tempered with him. Sort of moving him out of her way and bustling around. She snaps a few times, and he asks me if I want to go for a walk. YES! Leash on, and out of the house we go. As soon as we leave the house, Papa tells me, "Eddie, that Momma of yours gets a little crazy when her parents come to visit. The best thing for you and me to do is stay out of her way because nothing we can do or say will calm her down. Hang in there with me, my friend. We will get through this."

We arrive home and Momma is sitting calmly reading something and barely notices us. I walk over and hop on the couch next to her. She stops what she is doing and loves me and then quickly exclaims, "Oh Eddie, you are shedding! Look, there is hair everywhere." I look up at Papa and he winks at me. I remember what he said earlier and nestle in closer to Momma. She loves me some more and we end up taking a nice nap together.

The next morning, I awaken to more franticness. Mom is moving so fast and giving Papa orders. Papa patiently listens and goes about doing what he wants to do. He does get things done, and in his own time, not Momma's. This seems to irritate her. She seems to be annoyed today at everything.

Her and Papa leave me alone and they go off somewhere. Mom is very quiet. When they arrive home, they have two people with them and introduce me to them as Grandma and Grandpa Roesch. Mom says they have traveled very far to meet me. They are very kind to me, and Grandpa has a twinkle in his eyes as he gets down on the floor and talks to me. I sniff them, and they smell like

Momma. We have a nice dinner, and all snuggle in early. They are happy to be with us. I wonder if they are moving in.

The next day Papa and Grandpa Roesch leave the house very very early in the morning. Papa had bags packed, and these are different bags from his travel bags, so I know he is not leaving town. They smell stinky like fish.

Momma and Grandma Roesch and I are packed with a few items and heading out too. I am looking forward to this adventure. Momma is relaxed and she and Grandma are chatting a lot. Grandma Roesch walks like Momma...very heavy footsteps and I notice she talks often to herself like Momma does. They even have a similar smell.

We head down the road and I know where we are going, to that place in Girdwood with Momma and Papa's stuff. I have to walk up many flights of stairs and on a metal grate with holes in it. It hurts my pads, and I don't like being left alone there. You might say that I am not a big fan of the place. I do like hiking up the hills in their front yard and sniffing all the good sniffs.

Momma is happily showing Grandma Roesch the place and Grandma is oohing and ahhing over it. They left me for a short time. When I am there alone, I often bark. My hope is that they hear me and come back as I don't want to be left there.

When they come back, they have food and are laughing and chatting. I am hungry and a bit tired from barking. I would have preferred to hang out with Papa and Grandpa Roesch but no one asked me.

Luckily, we only spend one night there and then we go back home to meet up with the guys who are happily sharing stories of their fishing adventures. Papa spends time loving on me. They have been calling me "little man".

I like my Grandparents and have a fun time with them. The time seems very short and there are many tears when they leave. This is a bit confusing to me as Mom seemed so anxious about their arrival and now she seems to be so sad about their departure.

Human feelings are difficult to figure out. I get sad when they are sad and prefer them when they are happy.

CHAPTER 13

MOM TELLS A LIE

Momma has been chatting about a 'friend' for Eddie for several weeks and even brought me to meet a pup that has a similar body to mine. I like him and we zoom around as the humans laugh. I have been to see him 3 times now.

From out of nowhere, Mom and Dad receive a call or message somehow that that fun new friend is not going to be coming to live with us. I am ok with it because I prefer to be the only dog in the house. They do not seem to be listening to my wants and needs though, because Momma talks daily about different pups to Papa. Papa seems to be nonchalant and offers little feedback to Momma.

One day, Papa went off fishing and Momma and I stopped by his friend and boating partner's home where they were cleaning fish. Momma was chattering about an adoption clinic and Papa was a bit abrupt with her. He said, I am focusing on this fish right now and not sure why you are talking about a dog adoption clinic. Momma got upset and we said our goodbyes.

The next thing I know we are pulling into the parking lot of the place where I was dumped before Momma and Papa found me. I am very shocked and shaking a little.

Momma hops out of the car, and I watch her go right up to this big dog laying in a kennel. The people put a leash on her and Momma and the dog go walking off. All of a sudden, the back of the car opens and that dog hops in. The door closes and we pull out of the parking lot.

This dog has interesting smells and a ton of energy. She seems to be coming home with us.

We pull into our driveway and some of the ladies in the neighborhood greet us as the three of us head into our fenced yard. The ladies are oohing and ahhing over the dog. They tell Momma, "Don't worry, Bobby will love her."

I am thinking Papa is going to be surprised and I am not sure what Momma was thinking.

With that being said, Papa arrives shortly after. He comes in the front door and the new dog bounds over to him practically knocking him over. He is very serious and asks Momma who this is. Momma is laughing uncontrollably. She says this is our new girl, I went to the doggie adoption clinic today. Again, what was she thinking? Papa does not look amused.

He asks Momma "What happened? I thought we discussed no adoption clinic today?"

Momma is still giggling uncontrollably, almost like a nervous laugh, and responds, "My car just drove there on its own."

Oh boy, Papa looks less than happy.

Finally they both sit down to eat as this new dog is bouncing all over the house and Papa says, "I have 2 questions for you." Momma is still giggling however it is a different giggle from her happy giggle.

Papa says, "One; are there going to be more dogs? And 2; what were you thinking?"

Momma replies again that she is unsure and knows she should have talked to Papa and yet something deep inside her had her drive her car over and get this energizer young dog that she keeps telling to lay down to no avail!

I have a feeling things are going to get interesting. I am sorta siding with Papa on this one.

Momma, what were you thinking?

CHAPTER 14

ZENA FLAIR, THE FORCE

Momma moved her office to our home, and it is nice having her around. This new dog that they are calling Zena and Momma has been adding "Flair". She had another name that was sort of, well…not very suiting for her bundle of energy. And man oh man does she have some energy.

Momma and Zena are having some big old head strong challenges. They go round and round and Mom usually ends up crying. Mom has started running again and takes Zena with her. This is nice and gives me time to relax a bit and yet I do feel pangs of jealousy. I preferred being the only dog and this sharing thing has me a bit perplexed.

I am having trouble warming up to this Zena. She seems to want to cause trouble, often.

And now she is having this funky smell, that I kind of like. I am unsure why as she bothers me and yet I find myself following her around the house.

Momma tells Papa that she is in heat, and she is crying again. Papa is hugging Momma and telling her that everything will be ok. Zena is calm for once and very concerned about Momma's tears. She tells me she is worried that she is a bad dog, and that they are going to take her back. She says the family she was with threw her at the people where we found her that day Momma drove there.

Mom says to Papa, "What was I thinking?"

And my Papa is the sweetest man ever! He says, "You rescued this girl and look at her. You are like God to her. She loves you. We will get through this together." Momma falls into his arms and thanks him for loving her.

How did I get so lucky to live here? Maybe Zena is meant to be here with us. Maybe I can love her too, after all, she too got left behind.

CHAPTER 15

SHORT FUSE AND MISCOMMUNICATION

Momma and Zena are still in the figuring out stages. Zena has so much energy and Mom and Papa call her a 'force'. Zena tells me she wishes Momma knew how to communicate with her. She tries to figure out what she wants and gets frustrated, so she runs around with nervous energy. Meanwhile Momma starts off talking with Zena and it seems it often ends in yelling, and tears.

My take on the situation is they are both so alike. I tell Zena to behave, and what Momma is trying to tell her, and she often ignores me and does the opposite, which fuels Momma often into a full on rage.

The smell Zena had has gone away. They took her somewhere and she came back smelling like medicine and had to rest for a week. She cried in pain the first day and Momma quickly found help and gave her something for her pain. I kinda liked the smell she had and am not fond of this new smell but getting used to it and her.

I will admit that Zena adds zest to life at our home. There is rarely a day we don't go on an adventure walk or hike somewhere. I like this. Many days she bugs me and many days I feel like her companion, and she looks up to me for many answers.

Now, whether she listens, that is another story!

CHAPTER 16

THE MOVE TO THE FOREST

Something very odd is happening. First Momma and Papa took me far up on this hill to a log home. They introduced me to the lady that lives there, and I walked around the whole property with them. There are 90 something stairs that wind all the way down the property to another building.

Down below I meet a bigger dog that is not a dog but some other animal that doesn't have paws but hooves. I have seen his type before on the trails. He doesn't frighten me, but he makes a snorting noise and is eating hay. The nice lady says this is Buddy. Momma and Papa make sure I stay far enough away from Buddy so I don't get stepped on.

He has an interesting smell and I get scolded when I decide to take a bite of something yummy on the ground. Momma says, Eddie! Don't eat that!

The lady seems to like me and I love all the new smells of this property. I didn't like it as much as Momma and Papa, because the next thing

I know they are packing up all of our belongings which makes me incredibly nervous. Any boxes and movement of things makes me think about getting left behind. Before I know it, our boxes are being taken out of our home and put in this log home we just visited.

I am not sure how I feel about this.

CHAPTER 17

TRANSITIONS

Now, Zena Flair, Momma, Papa and I are spending the night in this log home with the funky smells. All of our boxes of stuff are here, and the smell feels off.

Zena seems to love it as she roams the property. We have tons of land to roam and a big fence. I am a fan of the fence because I can smell many critters big and small outside the gates.

There are trails outside the gates too and as a pack we explore them. Some of the smells, I have never smelled and am a little curious and a little uneasy of them.

I am letting Momma and Papa know that I am not thrilled to be here and am hopeful that we will be packing up from this adventure home on the hill and going home to our real home soon.

CHAPTER 18

PET SITTERS AND THE ADVENTURE HOME

Well, we are still at the Adventure home. There is no sign of us packing up and going back and I miss my old familiar smells. Zena, however, is loving every minute and assures me that she will keep the big black stinky critters on the other side of the fence with all the other critters too.

Every once in a while, Mom and Dad leave us with Hannah, Rebecca, Jamie, or a few other wonderful people that have come into our lives.

Mom doesn't think I know what is up before we get left behind, however, I know even before the 'frenzy' of her cleaning, doing laundry, changing the sheets, and telling me that she will be back 80 million times begins. I know they are leaving a week or more before they go. There is this feeling that Mom starts to put off and I pick up on it.

I am not sure where they go. Sometimes I think they go play with other pups as they often come home with those smells on them. Sometimes Mom has held and loved on these others. Papa rarely has. He knows that I know, and is very respectful. Mom on the other hand cannot discipline herself from them. I have witnessed her scooping up strangers into her arms and loving on them. I am always amazed. It is as if something takes over her and she forgets that I am watching. I like to think that she is pretending it is me when I was little because she did not have the chance to love on me then. I have sent signals to some of these pups in her arms to not get too comfy, they will not be coming home with us.

Currently, a bag is being packed and the Mom frenzy is happening. I am doing my best to be sad and not leave her side. She is moving so fast up and down the stairs. If she were a dog, it would appear that she was chasing a squirrel. She starts one task and quickly drops what she is doing to move on to the next thing and then back to the first thing. It is quite exhausting. Things are getting put in her pack, pulled back out, and then new items back in. This goes on for what seems like hours.

All of a sudden Mom says "POTTY! Come on guys, let's go outside!" Zena is there waiting with the ball. She is fast like Mom and always up for a good game of 'ball'. I am not in a hurry. I also don't want Mom too far out of sight, so I scurry outside in the cold with them.

Down 90 stairs we go to the barn. I put on an act, that we are going into the woods for a long walk. Mom does not have on her walking shoes, so I know this to not be true, but a boy can be hopeful. Mom frantically throws that darn rubber ball for Zena.

She runs, jumps, tackles alder tree stumps, and does whatever it takes to get that thing. Mom throws and throws and throws. I saunter around peeing here and there and eating a little moss now and then. Mom has tried to break me from grass-eating. She has listened to the guy who sticks needles in me. He says grass makes tiny cuts inside me, especially in my throat and tummy. I disagree and I miss eating grass. I have succumbed to nibbling on moss. I find it close to the trees on the ground. Mom has stopped me a few times and cannot seem to figure out what I am eating. She has even checked my mouth.

Back into the house, we go and Mom resume's her "frenzy". We get treats and I get the talk. On her knees, she says, "Eddie, I love you with my whole heart and soul and that is a lot of love. I will return to you. I always come home. Rebecca will be here with you. She is taking a vacation up here with you and Zena and loves you very much. Snuggle and love her." Urghhhh those words pierce my heart. Leaving, home soon, always comes home, blah, blah, blah.....my eyes are watering. Mom sees them and wipes away my tears. She goes about her tasks singing Eddie and Zena Flair, the best dogs in this house at this time. Bless her heart, she can't sing. Zena heads downstairs. She has very sensitive ears. I snuggle on the bed. I am so tired. We were up very very early watching Mom. I try to keep my eyes open, so she knows I am super sad.

Mom has recently started giving me shots once a week. Again, the guy who puts needles in me. He gave her this stuff. Says it is Vitamin B and will be good for me and my digestive issues. That and all this stuff that gets put on my food now. Mom quickly gives me a shot in my upper back. It itches and I make sure she knows that now I itch. She stops several times to scratch me and make sure I am ok.

Hugs and kisses and, "Be a good boy," and the door downstairs closes. Wheeewwwww, I made it, still on the bed. Sometimes we get booted out of the upstairs. Mostly when the bed has fresh sheets on it. I must have laid it on heavy because I am snuggled in. I hear the gate shut and her car drives away. My heart hurts. I would like to stay awake and be sad, but I am exhausted. Off I drift into a heavy slumber.

I awake to complete darkness. Is it the middle of the night, I wonder? I am hungry. Gosh....where is Mom? Where is Papa? Where is Zena? Barking begins from Zena. Guess I know where she is. I hear the front door open. Mom? Papa?! I rush downstairs hungry and hopeful. Hello Zena......that is a strange voice. I bark loudly advising that I am on patrol. It is Becca! "Hi, Eddie boy!!!" Oh her voice is like music to my ears.

All the lights go on and Becca is talking to us. I am happy to see her. "Do you both want to go potty? Outside you go!" Ohhhhh it is so cold out here. I hope she remembers to feed us.

Back in we go. Becca is giggling and chatting with us. Food is being put in our bowls. "I hope I am getting the right bowl for each of you. How are you both doing?"

"Just feed us", I try to convey.

Our food is put on the floor. Becca walks around a bit and puts her bag upstairs. She says she has to go back down the hill and will return in a few hours. What? Leaving us again? URGH! She leaves a bunch of lights on and off she goes.

We are left alone again. I eat only a little and Zena finishes off my food. This means I will be hungry soon.

Off to sleep, I drift again. Soon I hear the door open, and Becca is back. She has a friend with her, and I cozy up to both of them. We spend the night snuggling, watching movies, eating, and being. I do miss Papa and Mom but love Becca. She loves us, and I think she loves me a little more than Zena because I am on her lap.

On this particular trip, I was concerned on the first day. Becca came by the house late. She came in, fed us, and then left again. She came back several hours later and we snuggled.

In the middle of the night, the ground started moving. It does that often in this new house and this time is horrible! Becca awakes and tells us to follow her downstairs. We are having trouble walking. Becca grabs me and holds me and tells Zena to come next to her. We are under the bar in the living room. The rumble stops and we are all shaking.

Why does this happen? We did not sleep much after that, and my tummy was very upset. Becca kept reassuring us that we were all ok, but for some reason, I didn't feel too reassured.

In the morning we were all still a bit nervous, and Becca got up and got ready to go. What? You are leaving us here? Why? What if the ground rumbles again? Please, don't go. Don't leave us!

Off she went and my tummy hurt. Zena tried to comfort me although she was nervous too. I then heard a voice...."Eddie Bear, sweet Eddie Bear."

I know that I had chatted with this person before, but I was unsure. The voice was warm, reassuring, and kind. I say it is a voice when in reality it is more of a feeling I get. The feeling reminded me of the love from Bobby and Tracy. All of a sudden, I knew ALL was going to be alright. At that moment, my tummy stopped rumbling and I was relaxed.

Lee asked if it was alright to talk to me and that Momma and Papa sent her to make sure I was ok and happy. I am happy to tell her what is on my mind about this move, the property, and this unsettling ground!

Tonight, we are entertained by Becca singing and playing the guitar for us. I love when she sings, her voice soothes my soul. I kiss her hand as she strums her strings. She giggles to let me know that she likes it. Her friend snaps my photo, this I know to be a good thing from Mom always taking my photo. It helps me to forget about the unsettled ground below us.

In the daytime, we sleep in and get lots of cuddles and chats from Becca. We are walking through the woods and chasing squirrels. I am sniffing all the sniffs I can and leaving pee-mail for others to sniff. Z' ventures off as she always does, jumping, romping, roaming over shrubs, brambles, small trees, and whatever else is in her way trying desperately to get to the squirrel. I stay close to Becca as I sense a little fear in the deep woods. She knows the bears are still out and chats with her friend. I want to let her know she is safe with me. We don't see Z for a while and Becca calls her. Nothing. Darn her! Where is she, Eddie? Oh man, I send my signal to Zena. Get back here now!

All of a sudden, we hear her. Here she comes like a tornado! We can hear her, but not yet see her. There she is!!!! I smell something odd. She tells me she hurt herself. I smell blood but can't see it. Oh Z!! That's what happens when you chase those things blindly as you do. You are always getting hurt. Becca is happy to see her and does not notice that she is hurt. I try to communicate this to her but she does not pick up on it. She is just thrilled Zena did not take off too far.

We are home now and relaxing. Becca takes off our collars and is loving on us. What the?! What is that Zena?!! Oh no!!!! You are bleeding!!!! What the heck did you do? Oh no!!!!! I must let your Mom know. What a deep gash? Oh no! Are you in pain? What happened? It is a puncture and it's your nipple…what? Your nipple is gone! Oh geshhhh!!!! I am going to call the vet. What the heck happened? Are you ok? Poor poor girl.

Oh, brother……..she is fine. That is what she gets for chasing that darn squirrel and not obeying! Ghessshhhh…..she is fine. Hey, you can love on me a little more. Rub my tummy. She is ok. Off they go. The door shuts and I am alone. I wonder what just happened?

They come home a little later and Zena has that odd smell like medicine. All is fine or they both appear fine.

More snuggles, please!

CHAPTER 19

MURDERS IN THE YARD

It seems like no time at all and Mom and Papa are walking through the door again. I can always tell when they are coming home. I am not sure how, but I have a sense of their presence back to us before they even arrive. It always makes my soul feel warm to know of this. I love when we are all together snuggled in. There is no other place to be.

Momma seems unhappy, or rather agitated. I have felt this from her one other time before Zena Flair came to live with us. She gets sad. Sometimes she tells Papa that this feeling she gets is like a big dark cloud over her and she can't seem to shake it. It grabs a hold of her and rocks her to her core. She tries many things to overcome this including hanging out with her supportive women friends.

This feeling Momma is having makes me uncomfortable. I want her to be happy. I have a fear of getting sent away again. I know it isn't going to happen, but I still have it from time to time. More so the fear is that something will happen to Momma.

She gets told amazing things from people all the time and when this cloud comes over her, nothing anyone says matters. The feeling is real for her.

We all snuggle in early, and it feels nice and safe. We awake early and Momma and Papa sit at the dining room table. They don't usually sit here early in the morning. I am curious as to what is up.

They put their little box that they carry about with them in the middle of the table and a familiar voice comes out of it. I am trying to place her and then I know it is the lady that came to me last week, Lee!

Lee! I am so grateful that Lee can tell Momma and Papa my concerns.

Lee tells them that I am not happy in this new home and that I feel like the ground is unsettled. And about how I miss my old smells and that I have sensed murders in the yard.

Momma gets very upset and starts asking Lee questions, and Papa asks Momma to let Lee finish. Lee tells them that I am concerned about the smells in the yard and outside the fence and the ground.

Papa asks what we can do to make me feel better. I love Papa! Lee communicates for me that I would like some new balls with the old home smells. I love to squish tennis balls in my mouth and want the old smell.

Papa then asks Lee what day she communicated with Eddie and Zena and also what Zena thought of all this.

Lee says Zena agrees that the land is unstable and that there have been murders in the yard and also that she is watching over Eddie to keep him safe. She told Lee that she is having fun and loves to visit with her. She also asked Lee to come talk to her again.

Lee tells Papa and Momma the day and time that she communicated with us. The whole time Momma has been on the edge of her seat.

Papa tells Lee that the day she communicated with us was the day after a 7 point something earthquake. It was in the morning when Rebecca (the pet sitter) had left us alone as she had to go to work.

He also tells her that we have been having hundreds of quakes if not thousands since. Lee is in awe.

Papa precedes to tell her as Momma keeps mouthing to Papa, are we going to have to move? "Lee", Papa says, "the lady who sold us this house had chickens 40 feet from the house in a coop. A bear came in and killed them all and Eddie goes under the coop, which is now the woodshed all the time. We also have bears that walk by the fence as a game trail runs by both sides of our fencing. They are stinky and big."

Again, Lee is in awe and says, "That explains a LOT!"

Momma and Papa get off the phone, and Momma says "What if Eddie never likes it here? Can we move to Hawaii and leave this dark place?"

Papa says, "Yes, we will move if Eddie never likes it." Momma doesn't believe him and scoffs off. Papa tells us how good we are.

CHAPTER 20

MALE BONDING

I love hanging out with Papa and I get to go many places with him. A favorite is when we drive through any drive-through and I get lunches, treats, Puppachino's, and am told how adorable I am!

There are times when Papa picks up guys and they talk a lot about a lot of personal issues, problems, and joys in life. Papa seems to love helping others and I hear a lot of stories. I am told that this is all private between us guys and I like that I am included and trusted with these deep stories.

There is much laughter as well and sometimes these guys come to our home. Momma and Papa will have them for dinner and sometimes they stay overnight.

CHAPTER 21

CHRISTMAS PHOTOS

Oh man, does Mom love to take photos of us. I know how to pose and hold still. I do this when we are out and about - especially on walks when Mom yells, "SQUIRREL!" I know this is key to go into a full-on pose. Each time, Mom uses that little box she carries in her hand at all times to snap, snap, snap. I get tons of praise after a good pose. When Zena first came to live with us, she did not have a clue how to hold still. She believed and often still believes when Mom shouts "SQUIRREL!"…she runs off looking for them. A few times there is a squirrel, but nine out of ten times it is all to get the shot. Over the years, Zena has learned to stop and hold the pose.

Mom's favorite time of year is Christmas. I get completely perplexed each year watching her pull out several boxes with boxes inside and ginormous amounts of tissue paper and hanging things all over the house. Bless her heart, she cannot carry a tune although she tries and tries. I know she does not know the words because she fills in the verses blasting out Eddie and Zena Fa La La La La…...

Each Christmas she promises me we are not moving. She sees the worry in our eyes as the boxes come out. She says, guys, we are simply celebrating. When Papa is home, he will engage in belting out songs and helping Mom decorate. His task is always unpacking this cumbersome ginormous thing that resembles a tree and sits in the corner of the living area. It smells odd and yet the humans seem to love it. Papa seems ok with it, although secretly I know we both feel the same and think it is corny and would rather skip it altogether. It makes Mom happy, and we live to see her happiness shine. So we endure it.

Out they come. The hats and scarfs and barking stocking and Mom laughing. I love to hear her laugh. It is music to my ears, and I feel endeared to her when she laughs. So........I do whatever she wants which has meant posing in Santa hats and scarfs outside in the woods, sitting on a bench on the trail wrapped in scarves, and being told to "Wait...wait...Eddie...wait."

Today, Mom starts emptying her bag and out comes a Santa hat with a curly thing sticking out of the top. Mom? A grin appears on her soft face. Oh NO...No, NO .....on goes the hat pulled over my ears and eyes as I sit perplexed. I sit very still "waiting". She is giggling. I move a little and the hat tilts off. As quick as it tumbles off my head, Mom's fingers pull it back on over my ears and eyes, and giggling begins. "WAIT...Eddie, Wait! Good Boy! I love you Eddie Bear. You are such a good boy and sport!!!" She is giggling hard now. I am struggling to remain still. All of a sudden, the hat is off, and she bounds up the stairs laughing!!! Mom moves fast. I keep up with her from time to time, but tonight I watch from downstairs.

I hear her talking to Papa and laughing upstairs in the bathroom. I hear mine and Zena's names and Mom and Dad are coming down the stairs. Mom is still laughing and instructing Papa on how this is going to work. He has so much patience with her and usually does as instructed without asking many questions.

Mom moves the chair and grabs a scarf - I advise Zena, we are in for something, please follow my lead. "Eddie, get up. Eddie, UP." Mom is instructing me to jump on the chair. That chair is not stable and I am refusing this command. Mom is persistent. "Eddie, get UP!" I refuse and she picks me up and plops me on the chair. "Now, Zena, come here."

On goes the scarf around Zena's neck. Zena takes my instruction to sit still. It will be over soon. The quirky hat gets smooshed over my ears and eyes again and we are instructed to "WAIT". This seems to be taking longer than expected. I am hopeful treats and maybe even sleeping on their bed will be our "reward" for "waiting".

Mom is instructing Zena, Papa, and me. Again we have been shuffled around and the scarf put on Zena and the hat smooshed over my ears and eyes. Luckily this time I am sitting on the floor, not on that stupid wobbly chair. "WAIT, Wait, WAIT - GOOD boy and girl!!! Got it!" she shrieks! Papa is laughing now too and telling us how wonderful we are. Zena prances about as if she did something spectacular. I sit staring, catching their eyes, and looking into the kitchen. They are not getting my hint, so I wander into the kitchen and sit where I can see them. Again, make eye contact and direct my eyes to the 'treats'…."Come on, guys!" I lick my lips for the serious effect as they seem to be ignoring my demands.

Finally, Mom pulls herself away from that little box stuck in her hand and comes into the kitchen. "Good Eddie Bear!!! Want a treat?" Urghhhhhh I am thinking....yes, it took you long enough...ghesshshhhh. Zena comes into the kitchen and sits next to me. I must do all the work to get us these "treats", I am not sure why she even gets to get one. Food seems to always be the last thing on Zena's brain.

We get our "treats" and I get to snuggle on Mom and Papa's bed with them all night long. This Christmas photo session seems to be worth it.

When I think she is all done hanging all things, she takes it all down and packs it all up. This leaves me scratching my head. I must admit, I do like all the lights sparkling around the house and some of the presents that I get to unwrap. Other than that, I am clueless as to why this whole process happens each year.

CHAPTER 22

THE DOCTOR ACCIDENTALLY SHARES INFORMATION

Before Christmas Zena developed a limp. Mom and Papa seemed to be trying everything to help heal her leg. Zena told me she hurt and yet she would not stop chasing the ball, frisbee, or anything else that looked like a good thing to fetch or chase. The energy this gal has exhausts me. I know she is only 5 and ghessh!

The limp persisted and the doctors advised rest and no frisbee jumping. Mom is concerned and annoyed with it not healing. When Mom gets serious, we all get serious. We really like to be laughing, snuggling, and having fun and not so serious.

Mom and Papa started taking me to the doctor for my old injury from the moose, you remember the moose incident? I have developed bursitis in my left shoulder and sometimes I trip when walking. They take me to the doctor, where he inserts these tiny sharp things all over my body and head and sometimes my nerves twitch. I do not like it although after 30 seconds or so I get this euphoric feeling and have to lay down. I feel light and dreamy afterward and am told to relax the next day. While I am at the doctor's office, they tell Mom about trying the Ultrasound on Zena's leg and to bring her in. Mom is hopeful! Zena and I are hopeful!

The next day Mom takes Zena to the doctor for the ultrasound. Zena told me it hurt. I feel so bad and yet I am unsure what to do for her and her pain. When she rests, she passes out. I know something is up.

We move through our days walking, playing, and getting tons of snuggles …especially Zena. Mom rubs her leg, ices her leg, heats her leg, and asks Papa what he thinks daily. Each day seems to be filled up and it is very cold and dark right now, so we all snuggle in longer in the mornings and the evenings.

Mom is packing her bag and I get sad. She tells me Papa is staying home and that she will be back very soon. I have a weird feeling in my stomach about her leaving. I mean I always have it and yet this time it feels different.

Papa, Zena, and I are hanging out with Papa today. We stopped by the doctor's office for the dreaded pins in my neck experience. Papa is talking about Zena although I am not sure what he is saying. The doctor finishes up and takes the pins out of me and then pushes on my back. I feel relieved and relaxed and have all I can do to keep my head up. Out to the truck, we go, and Papa tells Zena to come with him. I am cold and sleepy and have that weird, odd feeling in my stomach again. I am trying to ignore it and wish Mom was here to comfort me. Where is she anyhow?

Seems like she has been away for too many sleeps this time. I am nodding off and trying to stay awake. I am unable to stay awake and am drifting off.

In the middle of the forest, I see and smell it! It is a large and completely filled dish of steak! I am running as fast as I can dodging the squirrels and other dogs. I am ahead of all of them and so close to the massive dish in the forest..............OH NO!!!! I feel the cold air and am jolted and stepped on. Papa puts Zena in the truck as she has stepped on me. Ghesssshhhh. Soooo rude and so cold and darn I was soooo close to that dish of steak! Papa? Papa? Papa, what is wrong? Papa is crying...oh no, Papa is crying. I rarely see him do this, oh no! Papa? What can I do? What happened, why? I feel out of control. My stomach hurts. I am unsure what to do.

We are still sitting at the Doctor's office in the parking lot. Papa is sobbing. Where is Mom? Mom? We need you now!

Finally, Papa turns on the truck and we slowly drive home. Zena is panting in my ear. I assure her as I always do when we are driving that we are ok. She worries so and is unable to relax. She gets slobber all over me and that is ok, I love her. I will move up to the front seat however to be closer to Papa and assume my position in the front. Papa? It is ok. I love you. Papa? I am hungry. Are we going home?

Yes, we are home! I am suddenly ravenous! I will herd him to make sure he remembers to feed me. Zena takes off to go do her thing, and check out the perimeter of the property with her nose. She never thinks about eating first, which baffles me. Papa is still sobbing and blowing his nose and I am reminding him by licking my lips and staring into his eyes that whatever he is feeling, my supper time is much more important at this very moment in time and not to be missed. Ummm...helloooo, Papa? Supper time. If I could whistle at him, I would. Instead, I sit at his feet staring into his soul.

Ahhhh, there, he's got it! My dish was in his hands and YES! It's supper time! I was feeling as if this was the night when I would surely not get my needs met.

Zena is at the back door now and Papa lets her in and tells her to eat her supper. She would rather play ball or pig or cow or tug than eat. Papa says, Zena girl, pretty girl, eat your supper sweetie. Zena settles down and eats. She comes over to me and burps in my ear. Ghesshhhh.... Zena? Do you mind?

Papa picks up his little box and starts chatting. I know he is talking to Mom. This is another thing the humans do that baffles me. I know she is there somewhere although I am unable to smell her or see her, yet he keeps talking.

Papa is trying to be strong and calm and he pauses and starts sobbing again. Oh Papa....if I could take your pain. I stare at him to let him know all is going to be ok. He is avoiding looking at me. Zena is staring at him now too. He seems to be holding back.

He seems surprised that Momma knows what he knows. He is mad at the Doctor for sending her an email by mistake telling her about this news.

I can hear Momma through the box crying.

CHAPTER 23

ANGELS OF COMFORT

One day leads to the next, at long last Mom is HOME!!!! She and Dad are standing in the kitchen crying. Zena and I are curious and sad too. I know it is because of Zena's leg. I smell it. Zena knows. Zena loves Momma so very much. She has told me that she is seeing the angels more and more frequently. They are a comfort to her, and she wishes Momma could feel their presence and comfort too.

Zena says they visit her often now when she is awake. She describes them to me as the most colorful fun rays of bright light that she has ever perceived. She attempts to sniff them and sometimes catches smells she has never smelled on earth. They are indescribable. Zena says when the Angels appear, she feels a warmth rush all over her body. She forgets about the throbbing of her leg. She is tempted to go with them as they are so loving and kind, but they have told her not yet. She tells me that Mom needs me now more than ever. I believe her and yet am saddened she is in so much pain and saddened that Mom is so very sad.

We all fall asleep in a big huge pile, just the four of us. I dream of that plate of steak in the woods and running so fast towards it.

CHAPTER 24

RESTLESSNESS

*Z*ena, tell me what you see? I am trying to see what you see or listen to the humans who are trying to see what you see. Actually, it is Mom trying to see what you see. "Zena, is it the angels? Are they here right now?" Mom desperately wants to see them as she massages Zena's leg, and water again flows out of her eyes.

I am not sure what is happening as the last few days or even weeks have been a blur of tears, laughter, hugs, all of us sleeping together, and more of the water out of the eyes. I am exhausted and overwhelmed and unsure of what to do from minute to minute.

Zena's leg smells more intense now and I assure her that I love her by letting her rest her head, her long legs, and even her paws on me. I pretend that it does not bother me and contain my sighs.

Often Zena sleeps in her own room downstairs where she can stretch her long legs and body out on the bed down there. The room is peaceful, cozy and, with the fan on, protected when the massive winds kick up and she freaks out. She will start out sleeping with us upstairs and then goes down to her room at night. I have been making her bed for her.

While she snuggles close to Mom, I hop off the bed onto her bed and arrange it for her. I work hard with my feet, adjusting the blankets how I think they would best allow her to be comfortable. Sometimes she copies me and will rearrange the bed. Mom and Papa giggle watching her. She is a bit clumsy and uses her teeth. Sometimes she is standing on the blanket she is trying to move around and then grabs it with her teeth. It won't move because, well, she is standing on it. She gives it her best effort and then clumsily plops down.

She is restless and I often wonder if that is why she goes downstairs, to not keep us all awake.

CHAPTER 25

ZENA IS DIFFERENT

Today is an interesting, very stressful day. Zena went very early to the doctor. Before she went Momma was on her knees a few times, and there was a big moose out in front of our house. Momma says they are her Spirit Totem Animal, always appearing when things are disturbing.

Mom cried and kept telling Zena things I could not understand. Momma is uptight and restless. She is currently pacing, and I really just want a walk. Does she not see me sitting here, ready to help take her mind off everything? Hello, Mom…ummmm excuse me, can we please go for a walk?

Hmmm….It seems like it is not going to happen and I am bummed out. I guess I could nap, or I could continue watching and following Mom around the house. She is very intense.

Papa is home now, and they are talking. Papa took Zena's bed in the spare room apart and put the mattress on the floor. This is concerning. Ghessh …so often I wish I knew what they were up to and why. I am puzzled by this one and I am hanging very close to both of them.

Mom and Papa think Zena is different, but I only smell and see the same, Zena. Mom cries often and loves Zena so very much.

Zena returned home from the doctor with 3 legs instead of 4. Momma and Papa were concerned about me feeling differently. I, however, was glad for the smell on her leg to be gone.

We walked outside together (yes, she is walking!) and I accidentally got under her and smelled her stump. It has a curiously odd smell of things that hurt my nose.

Mom and Papa are giggling as they watch us and I hear my name 'he' so I know they are talking about something I have done. This makes me happy, to see them happy after all the tears!

This night is not a fun night at all. Mom stays downstairs in Zena's room with her. I hear Zena's cries all night. Before Papa goes upstairs, I am licking tears off Zena's eyes and Mom has a warm towel on her face. Zena has tears running down her face. She is distressed.

Mom is crying. Papa and I go upstairs and within minutes Papa and I fall fast asleep. I awoke to Mom shouting for Papa. She is shouting so loud. I am paralyzed and unable to move. Papa is sound asleep. Mom is standing at the bed. "Bobby! Bobby!" Papa jumps up. Mom is crying and going on and on about Zena.

Papa assures her somehow and off he goes. Mom snuggles in with me holding me tight. I love her so very much, so I let her squeeze and squash me. I feel smothered and have all I can do to not push and pull away. I finally sigh. A big sigh to let her know, I need some space. I am wet from her tears and so very sleepy as I am drifting somewhere deep in the most luscious grass. It is so soft. I am so comfortable, and the warm sun is on my fur. Oh, I am so light and floating in the wind on the grass. I see Zena. She is the same Zena and even tells me she is not in pain anymore.

The first three days home were a little tough for all of us. Zena wants to play, run and jump for the frisbee. Mom and Papa are keeping close tabs on her and her leash. Zena wants to be free and untethered. She tells me she wishes to run like the wind... even though the wind terrifies her. She likes to sniff and run with all the yard critters. She wants to soar with the angels, and she has told me that she is worried about leaving Mom behind. Mom is scared of Zena going to the angels. She loves her so much here on earth and does not understand we will never be far apart. I know this and am unable to convince Mom. Papa knows this too and I think he uses words to help Mom understand. Oh, the questions Mom has! I sigh at night often letting her know to be still as she chats. Papa does make her laugh lots. Zena and I love when they laugh. We love to be liked together when they are laughing.

Today Zena is going to the doctor's office again. This time when she arrives home, she has a funny odd odor to her, and she is very lethargic. She is telling me about the "colors" that she is seeing, and I have no idea what she's talking about as this is not one of my "words". I desperately want to connect to the colors she tells me about. It is dreamy and luscious and sounds delicious too. She drifts off to a deep sleep moving all four legs (3 legs and one stump). I know she is chasing the tasty 'colors'.

Papa is home early today and takes us across the street into the woods. Zena flies down all the stairs to our down-below area, pulling Papa quickly along. Mom would be laughing at how fast Papa and I are moving as she claims we are "strollers". Papa and I are ok with going slow. He "gets" me and he knows I like to sniff all the sniff. He is often doing things on the little box they both carry with them at all times. We sort of have an agreement. Doing our guy things, no chatter. No fast-moving. However, today Zena has energy galore, and we seem to fly down the stairs into the woods. I am happy and feel like all is well and right today.

CHAPTER 26

MY HEART HURTS

Zena seemed to enjoy each day as if she would live forever here with us on earth. Mom rubs her at night, and over time a new lump on Zena develops. We were all holding on to each and every day with Zena Flair. Loving the moments and knowing that she would soon be making her way to the angels who were visiting often.

Mom catches Zena watching them floating above her. Zena has no worries about anything when the angels are close by. However, if the wind blows, she is terrified!

When Momma talks about the lump growing and intensifying, Papa tells her to please leave it alone. Zena continues to play, run, and enjoy each and every single day.

The pain started getting worse. Even though Zena keeps going, we can see it in her eyes and in her body. Back-and-forth to the doctor we go. Each time Momma or Papa brings home more and more pills for her.

One doctor even came by our house. Tears. There are many, many tears. Momma is crying uncontrollably and so many angels are here.

They show themselves to me sometimes and I love to see them. They are so very colorful and filled with love. It's hard to describe what I actually see, however I know from deep inside when they're present. A warm softness fills the room. I like having them close and I feel safe from the critters outside in the yard.

I know Zena likes them, although sometimes I think she gets confused as they dance above her head. She also has this incredible urge to be with them and yet she is worried about leaving Momma.

The bond Momma and Zena have for each other is so intense. It is very hard to watch both of them in so much pain.

The pain becomes so intense that it seems the only position for Zena to be comfortable is when she is standing.

Momma and Papa are having a very deep conversation and the tears are flowing. Mom has been up off and on for two nights with Zena. It's hard to watch this. Zena can't get comfortable and yet still wants to run and fetch the ball. How is this even possible with the pain she is in?

Papa says to Momma, it is time. I am not so good at understanding all their words and yet I understand what this means. It is time for Zena to be with the angels.

I know when we all get into the car that this is the last time that we are all going to be together here on earth. Zena knows too, and she is filled with sadness. She asks me to stay close to Momma and

Papa over the next few months, especially Momma. She is worried about Momma.

Zena knows that she helped Momma to overcome some very dark times, and she wants me to reassure her that I will fill in. I tell her I will do my best to keep Momma from revisiting the darkness.

I let her know how much I love her and that the angels will restore her body. She will be free from pain, and we will always be connected to her in our hearts and souls. I ask her if she will send us a message when she meets the angels. She says she will do her best and she too loves me and Papa and Momma very much. She knows we will always be connected.

CHAPTER 27

EAGLES

We arrive back home without our beloved Zena Flair. The house feels like something is missing. There is sadness in the air. We are all in the living room and I am laying on the floor listening to Momma and Papa, and all of a sudden, SHE APPEARS! Zena Flair is on the stairs looking at me! I stand up and look at her. Momma and Papa stop talking and look at me and then at each other.

Eddie, what do you see? Is that Zena Flair? Zena tells me that she is in so much peace and free from pain. She says the angels are guiding her to beauty as she has never witnessed on earth. Mom and Papa keep asking me what I am staring at and I wish they would stop, as I am having a conversation with Zena Flair.

Zena tells me not to be sad and to help Momma and Papa move forward with happy memories. She is Free! And then she disappears.

I lay back down and still Momma is asking me questions. I am not sure why she didn't see Zena. I did and I am at total peace. I know

I will have my job cut out for me to help Momma and Papa …especially Momma, be at peace.

Papa then says he is going to go to the office and "Eddie, be a good boy and stay with Momma." He hugs us both and heads out the door.

Momma is lost. She is talking to me and telling me how much she loves me and squeezing me. Her tears are soaking my neck and I remember the promise I made to Zena, so I stay in position next to Momma.

We go upstairs and into Momma's office. I am as close as I can get to her when this screeching starts outside.

Momma gets on the floor and looks out the window. I am trying to look to see what the racket is all about.

There are two big eagles on top of the tallest trees outside Momma's office, screeching back and forth with each other. We are in awe!

Then one flies right by the window and the other one follows.

Momma says, Eddie, I think that was Zena Flair giving us our sign that she is ok.

Course, I didn't need a sign as I just saw her on the stairs, and I am grateful she was able to give Momma a sign to ease her heart!

CHAPTER 28

ZENA VISITS

The days, weeks, and months after Zena Flair joined the angels are very quiet. Momma misses her so very much and often breaks down in tears.

She shares Zena's story with people from all over the world and receives cards, letters, and gifts from many. Zena Flair is known as a Warrior and many people witnessed her strength and determination.

Momma seems edgy with Papa often. This saddens me. I talk to Zena often about this as she visits me.

What I appreciate is all the snuggles and extra love from both Momma and Papa. I liked the stillness as Zena Flair was a force in our home…I mean I miss her soul. I also feel her presence within our home and on the property.

When Eagles soar above, Momma and Papa watch them and say, "Hello Zena Flair." Even when we walk with Momma's friend Bev, Bev says hello to Zena when an eagle soars above.

They fly close over our home often.

The stillness is getting to Mom. She likes to hike and often goes to climb mountains alone. Bev goes with her sometimes which she loves, and also, she loves solo time.

I wish I could go with her as a way to help her feel safer out there, but my legs and body are not up for those kinds of hikes anymore.

The last time she dragged me to the top of Flat Top Mountain we were hiking over boulders that were huge. This was before Zena Flair. Momma went the wrong way on the backside of the mountain and had to lift me over these monster things. When we finally made it to the top, she asked a nice lady to take a photo of us. I walked away from Momma because I was so annoyed at her for making me do that climb. We took the easy way down and that was the last time I climbed a mountain. Zena Flair took my place after that!

It saddens me to see Momma's soul so restless and missing Zena so. She took me on gentle hikes, even to the back of a mountain not too far up that mountain. I know, she doesn't take me too far. I also know her soul needs to go far. Momma has a lot of energy, and it helps her darkness stay away when she can move and move often!

CHAPTER 29

A GERMAN SHEPHERD?!

One night as Mom and Papa lay in bed with their little boxes in their hands, Mom said, "Hey Papa, listen to this, German Shepherd/Malinois puppy dumped at the pound. It is begging someone to help this pup out and go get her!"

I am certain that this was talk of a puppy. Papa replied, "It is after 10 PM, let's talk in the morning." I had a feeling that our lives were about to change from the stillness.

I had a restless night tossing and turning.

CHAPTER 30

WHY MUST THINGS CHANGE?

Somehow, I have gotten to be an old man dog. Although I still feel like I am young, my body is starting to ail me. I have developed a chronic cough, so Mom and Papa have taken me to the doctor to run every test and to figure out what is wrong, to no avail. They even used a little steam machine for weeks on me two times a day. It is annoying, as I have to sit and inhale it for what feels like forever.

In the midst of my growing old and feeling achy, Papa has awarded me the title "Office Dog". Most days, I get to go to work with him and protect his office. Mid-day we walk, and I run errands, often gathering treats along the way. I even go inside the place where he sits, and they cut his hair. They love me there and they always give me treats.

Most places we go they love me and ask the same old question in a loud voice, "What is he, he is so cute?"

More and more I have difficulty hearing Mom and Papa's voices. I see their lips moving, but nothing comes to me. They have been teaching me hand signals. Sometimes, though, I can hear them clear as day.

I am ok either way. It is quiet and calm ….except for our new addition, Chance Z. She made herself known to us as a puppy. Mom and Papa brought her home one day with a funny smell.

I was less than thrilled as this kind of dog is one of the only kinds of dogs that I have never been keen on at the dog park.

She greeted me in my yard. I was not a happy boy.

She came up to me all loopy and doopy and had that medicine smell to her.

Momma and Papa "Said she is a German Shepherd/Belgian Malinois Mix, Eddie, and your new sister."

I wonder if they can see me roll my eyes at them in complete disbelief.

Oh, brother, I thought! Just when I was liking having Mom and Papa all to myself. Why, oh, why do we have to have her here with us?

Momma and Papa go around and around with different names to call her. She has a name and yet it seems very unfitting for this fearless girl. I have a few choices of my own, but they don't ask me my opinion.

Mom likes to sit still in silence usually in the morning, with her coffee. Today she is sitting still, and suddenly jumps up from where she is seated and runs into the bathroom where Papa is getting ready for work. "CHANCE Z!" she yells.

He says, "What are you talking about?"

Momma exclaims, "Second Chance for her and me because I had lived with a German Shepherd before and did a terrible job training her and so we both get a second chance! And Z for Zena Flair! We can call her Chance Z!"

Of course, Papa goes along with this name as Momma is overjoyed with excitement.

They proceed to break out in song and dance which they sometimes do. Papa starts making up funny songs about Chance Z and we all dance together. I love when we are doing this together, even if she is doing it with us. Chance Z seems to be giggling in delight.

CHAPTER 31

SLEEPLESS NIGHTS

Her first night was a success. We all sleep soundly through the night. This isn't so bad. Oops, I spoke too soon. It is night two and it's not peaceful at all. Chance Z is up and she's a full bundle of energy. And we are all awakened by her presence. Up and down all night long.

Again, I am wondering, why do things have to change?

One day seems to roll into the next and Momma and Papa have incorporated a big box upstairs in our bedroom for Chance Z. I have gone in it and sniffed it out to make sure there are no hidden treats. It is an interesting box and it's huge!

Chance Z gets asked to go in it before we go to sleep or start out in it. Many nights Momma gets up and lets her out and then we are awake off and on. I am tired. She is so young and has so much energy.

I wonder when I will get to rest a full night again.

CHAPTER 32

SIT, COME, STAY, SPIN, REWIND - TREATS!

Today this wonderful lady, Kar, came over. She likes me and gives me scritches. Kar not only loves me, but she also has pockets filled with treats! She gives them out generously and I adore her!

Kar is telling Mom and Papa that they had better spend the time training Chance Z, otherwise, life would be insane.

Here we go.

They call it "doggie 'crack'". Momma and Papa carry these little bags around their waists and fill them with tiny treats that Papa cuts up. They ask Chance Z to do things for them, and I get to have the treats too for tagging along. They call me the assistant coach. I am ok with it because this stuff is so delicious. They give them out all through the day, all while asking her to do things. Sit down, come, and a few things I do not understand like spin and rewind where she goes in circles.

Touch is an interesting one. They want us to touch their hands with our noses, and I do this new thing because I get the crack! I refuse to spin and rewind though.

This little practice calms Chance Z down and then she passes out in a major sleep coma. They have started calling her CZ for short and putting her in her box many times during the day. She comes out of it a little calmer.

Things may be working out with CZ here.

CHAPTER 33

FEELING LEFT OUT

Today, Momma, CZ, and I load up in her car and go to the nice lady, Kar's house. CZ and Momma get out and I am told to wait. I am wondering why CZ gets to go in and I am betting that she is getting more of the crack. I feel a bit left out. Momma comes back to the car without CZ and we leave. Momma says we will come back later and get her. This is odd.

We return home and it is so peaceful. I sleep soundly all day as Momma works and moves around the house. I awake to CZ standing staring at me. She conveys that it is supper time. I am shocked, as I am very timely when it comes to my 5 pm supper time. Momma and Papa joke about my watch on my paw.

I like the quiet and peace in the house during the day. She comes home at night and is pretty tired. She is very smart, although I am a bit bummed when they give her lots of attention.

Chance Z also loves to get in the water. Yuk! This is so confusing to me to watch her jump in creeks, lakes, and puddles.

Every puddle she can find she lays in. The muddier the better! She even jumps in the tub, which baffles me to this day.

When Momma and Papa teach her things, I am teaching her manners. She is mouthy and I will have none of that! I let her know this is unacceptable and to knock it off. I have had to growl and snap at her a few times to discipline her. She also likes to herd me. Yes, me! This is annoying as I am the chief herder of the family, at the park and other places, as well as the chief snuggler!

Mom is spending oodles of time with Chance Z. Walking, and tons of training. Chance Z mimics Mom's energy and recently Mom got told to "slow her roll" by CZ's trainer'. Mom has always had a bit of a high vibe and it sometimes makes me nervous.

CHAPTER 34

BIG SHAKER

It is cold outside today and Momma and Papa are in the bathroom getting ready for work chatting away, when all of a sudden, the ground starts shaking uncontrollably! We all run downstairs as fast as we can.

CZ freaks out and tries to throw herself through a window! Papa has to hold her. We are standing and the shaking subsides. We stand there for a minute and BAM! We start shaking again.

Momma is saying words that I don't hear often, and she starts to cry. Papa keeps reassuring us that we are going to be ok. He tells us to stay still for a few minutes. CZ is a wreck!

Minutes go by and the shaking has subsided. There are several areas in the house where things are broken. Momma and Papa start to clean up the mess when Papa says, "I am going to check on Auntie M."

Momma says, "WHAT?! We are all going with you." We all pile into his truck. The ground is still moving, smaller shakes now.

We head down the hill to our favorite Auntie M's house. We arrive to find her, okay, and things are broken throughout her house. She has no electricity. CZ gets left in the car because Auntie M is watching a few dogs.BOOM! Another big shake and Papa, Momma, and Auntie M grab hands and pray. I was sure it was the ground at our house that was unsteady, but it is at Auntie M's, too.

We spend quite a bit of time here and then head to Papa's office. There are things broken there too. The ground rumbles and rolls a few more times loudly.

CZ is beside herself, and we are all consoling her.

The shakes seem to last forever on this day. One after another and Momma is miserable as is CZ.

CHAPTER 35

ADVENTURE HOME ON WHEELS

Momma thinks it would be fun to load us all up with food, water, snacks, toys, and bedding and go for an adventure. And so she does and so we do! Off we go on our first adventure!

I like to sit in between Momma and Papa. Well, I take that back, my preference is in the passenger seat that Momma insists on sitting in. They put me in between them on the floor with pillows, and blankets and try to get me up high enough to see out the window. It does not work, and the floor gets hot. Also, CZ likes to crowd me on the floor. She moves around, as usual, trying to settle.

At one point, I am so uncomfortable, Momma picks me up and puts me in her lap. I am very uncomfortable sitting like this, and yet I love the air from the open window on my face. I stay like this on her lap for as long as possible. I like to see the sights going by and I like the extra attention.

We stopped at our first spot near a beach with sand. CZ and I get to run and play on the beach. The sand feels so good on my pads. CZ is running into the very cold ocean and hopping over the waves. She is a bit nuts!

This is a fun adventure although it is very quiet like in our home in the woods. The only difference is that there is the ocean, and we are something like a car but much bigger.

The bed is much smaller than our big huge bed at home. Momma makes me stay on the floor and I get cold at night and let her know that I would like to sleep snuggled with them. Momma lifts me up in between her and Papa. We awake in a big pile, the four of us snuggled tightly in.

Today we do more adventuring and sightseeing. CZ and I get to run and play on new trails and there are many new sniffs. Some of the sniffs are like the sniffs outside our fence at home. Momma is cautious for us not to go too far. She is not a fan of those critters with the smell either.

CHAPTER 36

TIME TO PASS THE TORCH

Over the past 3 years with Chance Z living with us, I feel like I have taught her all I can. I have taught her manners, kindness, how to stand up for herself, and most importantly how to love.

The relaxing part does not come easy to her, and she will need to continually work on this on her own and with the help of Momma and Papa. Mostly Momma though, as Papa knows how to be calm and relax. Mom has a bit harder time in this area.

I am living my best life at 14 years old when I am writing this ending. I go to work with Papa when I want to, and I let him know when I want to stay home and rest. I am on a strict diet that they tell me keeps me in good shape. I question this diet daily! I walk a half-mile to a mile most days and I love to rest on all the comfy blankets and pillows Momma has for me.

It is a good life and Momma and Papa have kept their promise to help me when my hips are weakening.

They often help me up and down the stairs and when I don't want help with the 90 stairs down the property, I go under the stairs up the hill. The snow makes it a tough climb and I am still climbing.

Thank you for reading my story. May your life be filled with a furry companion and oodles of love and laughter.

xo

Eddie the Dog

ACKNOWLEDGMENTS

A s one of Eddie's humans, his Momma, I wish to thank my dearest partner and husband, Bobby, the one who supports all my endeavors and gently pushed me to finish Eddie's story. It took 10 years and Bobby loved and encouraged me through all of them.

Thank you AARF for that night filled with non-coincidence that introduced Bobby and me to dearest Eddie. We appreciate all that you do for rescue dogs.

Thank you to Friends of Pets for connecting people to dogs and their forever homes!

Thank you to all my mentors and spiritual advisors (you know who you are and I love you) for encouraging me to keep writing! Thank you for buying this book. xo ~ *Tracy*

Eddie wants to thank his amazing pet-sitters, and a special thank you to Jamie & Kyle, and Jedi who took us on grand adventures when Momma and Papa were out of town. Thank you for all the fun videos of us enjoying adventures in Alaska.

Thank you to all my grandparents for loving me when I got to see you. Momma Holly, Grandpa and Grandma Roesch, Grandpa Orie and Grandma Phyllis. Thank you to all my Aunts and Uncles and a special visit with cousins Luci and Jack. Thank you to all the spiritual advisors that love and support my humans. Esther thank you for your gentleness. To all the men in Papa's life that I got to know and love. Thank you, Auntie Marcia, Auntie Janice, Auntie Karen and Bev and beloved Molly.

I know Eddie and I are missing soooo many dear friends and relatives that got to be a part of Eddie's story. Please know we love and thank each and every one of you!

ABOUT THE AUTHOR

racy Roesch Williams is Eddie's human Momma and transcriber of Eddie's story. Tracy lives in Anchorage, Alaska in a log home surrounded by mountains and nature with her husband Bobby and their two rescue dogs, Eddie and Chance Z. Tracy is an Executive Life Coach and Business Consultant with *Alaska Tracy* (www.AlaskaTracy.com).

She uses her Vision Mapping Framework to guide people on their journey to achieve and live a peaceful rewarding life…filled with LOVE! Follow Tracy (Alaska Tracy) for inspirational tools, tips, and oodles of photos of Alaska, wildlife, and her travels.

Made in the USA
Middletown, DE
06 May 2022

65356527R00076